SECOND TIME AROUND

Joshi Carroll

ISBN: 978-1-64184-294-5 (Paperback)
ISBN: 978-1-64184-295-2 (ebook)

DEDICATION

To my SugarPop, who supported me by giving up
a cruise so I could write this story.

ACKNOWLEDGEMENTS

I've always wanted to own a bookstore. Since my partner and I have discovered we like RVing, I thought creating a portable bookstore would be fun and a great way to make extra money. It seemed apropos to write a story about living in an RV park and selling books. Oh and of course, woman meets woman was important especially women who are over the age of fifty.

I want to thank Tom Bird for helping me get over the hurdle of writing my first book and helping me get through the process of self-publishing. The process has been easy and fun for my first novel. He provided me with a style editor and copy editor, which saved me a lot of headaches.

Thank you to my friends who supported me through this endeavor and especially, my friend Janelle who meets with me and listens to my story ideas. She gives me great advice and is always there when I need a sounding board.

Getting the right cover design was important to me and a big thanks to my illustrator John Rose. He listened to what I wanted and produced my vision without us having to spend a lot of time going back and forth.

Finally, I am eternally grateful to my fantastic fans who have been waiting patiently for me to get this book done. They give me a purpose to keep on writing.

GONE TOO SOON

"Maddie is not dying!" Austin Stevens exclaimed out loud trying to convince herself this nightmare wasn't true. In her mind, saying Maddie wasn't dying out loud might not make the situation real, as if the last few months were a bad joke. She didn't want to hear the incessant beeping any longer.

The chirping had been background noise for three days. *How could this be happening? I was living my ideal life a year ago. I had a loving partner. We had a wonderful home and then she complains of a backache that won't go away. Before I know it, I'm going back and forth to the doctor with her, she's been diagnosed with stage four pancreatic cancer. The doctor tells us there was no way to catch it, Maddie probably had the disease for a while, long before the pain made her see a doctor. The doctor told us we needed to start treatment right away. We didn't have time to catch our breaths and now, Maddie is never going to be able to catch her breath,* Austin thought as she stared at the skull-like visage of the love of her life.

Seeing her partner on death's door made Austin want to scream or beat the wall or cry until she couldn't cry anymore. Her Madelaine had been so beautiful. Austin had called her "The Indian Princess" because of the way she looked. She had worn her hair long, usually braided down her back, which had accentuated her high cheekbones. Her eyes had been expressive and full of life. She had been a couple inches shorter than Austin and when they entered a room everyone had looked at them.

They had fit together. Their love story was material for a bardic ballad, if such a thing still existed. Everyone always commented how jealous they were because they wished they had the kind of love evident in both women's eyes when they looked at each other.

Austin hated the scent of death. The smell pervaded the air in the bedroom. The aroma of antiseptic along with the musk from the lover was almost too much. She thought if she brought her partner home the smells would go away, but they followed, seeping into every nook and cranny of their bedroom.

The smell ruined the ambiance Maddie had worked so hard to create in their love nest, as she called it. Their bedroom was decorated with rich tones of royal blue and purple. The walls had been painted a light shade of blue, creating a calming atmosphere. The bed had the deeper jewel tones because Maddie wanted Austin to feel as if she were royalty when they went to bed.

There was no comfort when she looked at the bed. All she saw was her dying partner hidden away from the world. The frustration of not being able to do anything to help Maddie added to the overwhelming need to run away. Maybe if she ran away, time would stand still, and her lovely partner of thirty years wouldn't die, and they could go back to pretending like they were a royal couple surrounded by comfort.

Austin had tried to maintain the sense of comfort even after they realized Maddie wasn't going to get well. She had teased Maddie about bringing her meals in bed and fluffing her pillows to make her comfortable. Maddie had laughed and told her not to forget she was the queen of their world and should be treated as such.

Madelaine Williams was a trouper, doing what needed to be done. Getting the chemo and taking all the crappy medicine the doctor wanted her to take, dealing with the poison flowing through her body. Austin scoured the internet each night looking for ways that would make the treatments easier for Maddie, but nothing helped.

They had tried herbal teas, smoking marijuana, and many other home remedies. After going to the chemo appointments for six months with no improvement, Maddie had said "I'm done, no more. I feel worse putting this crap in my body than I do without it."

"What! What do you mean? We have to keep trying baby, I know this is tough, but you're going to get better, I know it." She said, but her partner was resolute. No more chemo, no more drugs. They weren't working and she wanted to spend her last days loving Austin. Not in front of the toilet, which was where she spent most of the time after her treatments, or sleeping, because the drugs sapped her energy. They made her miserable and Austin realized that all the work she had been doing to try to help Maddie wasn't going to make it easier for partner. She loved Maddie so much and although she knew this would be the beginning of the end, she accepted what her partner wanted.

Austin's father was with her when Maddie made the decision to stop the treatments. After she had put her partner to bed, he held his daughter while she cried, giving her love and support, but she knew it was difficult for him as well. He loved Maddie as much as Austin loved her and he had cried along with his daughter. Father and daughter were distraught, knowing they could do nothing to help the one person in their lives who gave them balance. Austin as her partner and her father as another daughter he could love unconditionally.

Buckston Stevens was a strong man, but the death of his daughter's partner had almost done him in. He had loved Madelaine Williams from the moment Austin had brought her home. She was vivacious and full of life. She always had a smile on her face and the way she looked at Austin made him realize she was a keeper. She had handled Austin in a way that brought her back to him, when he thought she was lost. His gratitude and appreciation for Maddie never faltered and grew as the years went by.

Having been raised in a Southern Baptist household, he had struggled at first with their relationship, but she won him over. Maddie had been subtle in her quest to get Buckston's approval. She never confronted him or made him feel like his opinion was wrong. She accepted him and his judgments. Austin would get angry with him and his attitude, but Maddie would remind her that he was her Father and he needed her. He was forever grateful for her patience and kindness. When they found out she was sick, he went home the first night and cried.

Her Father had supported Maddie's decision and had arranged for her to spend her final days at home with Austin. Hospice came in twice a day to check on her, but her time to leave this world was getting closer. *I love her so much. Why is this happening to us? I don't want to have to start over. For God's sake, I'm fifty years old. I thought we were going to grow old together, I thought we would both go peacefully in our sleep.* She had imagined going to bed when they were in their nineties, shutting their eyes and never waking up -- together, not separately.

~~~~~

Maddie's body had begun the process of shutting down. Every now and then Austin would hear a gasp as her lover's lungs struggled to get enough air. She had been warned by the hospice nurse that when Maddie's body began the process of dying, she would likely hear the "death rattle," as it was called in layman's terms.

On the day Maddie died moments after the hospice nurse came in to check on her, Austin knew her love was no longer with her in spirit. Maddie had become unresponsive. No matter how much Austin talked to her and touched her lovingly there was no movement, no clasping of hands, no opening of eyes, nothing.

Austin was gazing out the window because she couldn't stand to look at her love any longer. Suddenly a tiny, yellow butterfly appeared. At first, Austin thought it was caught in a spider web because it seemed to be floating in the air as if the insect was caught on the spider's silk, but after closer inspection, she saw a barely visible push of the wings. The moment felt as if the butterfly was waiting for something. The tiny insect floated in the air for what seemed like hours but was only minutes.

Maddie's eyes flickered open for the briefest moment. She looked at Austin and she smiled at her. Her eyes twinkled as they always did when she was telling her she loved her and then they went blank. The butterfly flew off at the same time. Austin knew Maddie's soul had left with the butterfly. *I look at her now and all I see is a body without any kind of life. It's still going through the motions of living, but there's nothing in her heart. I know it's time let her go.*

"It's okay, Honey, you can go, you don't have to hang on any longer. I'll be okay. I'll miss you so much, but I know you're ready, just go. I'll see you one of these days and we'll sit on our porch and laugh and joke about our life together."

The time between gasps was getting longer. It was difficult for Austin to listen to the crackly wheezing. She wanted to reach out and shake her partner and tell her to stop fooling around. She wanted her to open her eyes and laugh and say she was just kidding. She wanted so much. She wanted her love. She wanted their life. She wanted her Maddie to be okay.

Austin looked at her partner who was so robust in life but had been reduced to a small, frail entity. She had lost weight as the cancer ate away at her body. Her hair had fallen out and had grown back curly and white. Austin tried to remember her as she was before the disease took away her attributes.

Maddie was buxom for a small woman, which she attributed to her Mother's side of the family. Austin's partner, when describing her physique, had said she had extra meat on her bones. Her hair was dark brown and had started to show streaks of gray. Her chocolate-colored eyes were almond shaped, and Austin called them "Almond Joys" because they reminded her of the candy bar. Austin could always tell how she was feeling by looking into her eyes.

Austin had loved every bit of her and had struggled when the weight began to slough off her. She had watched her partner waste away and tried to hide her anger at the disease, but she was not always successful. Maddie would hold her and tell her it was okay to be angry, she was mad, too. She would joke about it taking her so long to build the cathedral that was her body and a stupid disease was tearing it down one block at a time. Austin would laugh and everything would be okay for a while.

~~~~~

A few months before Maddie died, they had been lying in bed holding each other. They had not made love since they found out about Maddie's disease and were arguing. Maddie wanted to make love and Austin was worried.

"Dammit, Maddie. I love you more than anything, but I don't want to hurt you, or god forbid make you worse."

"That's the stupidest thing I've ever heard from you, Austin Lee. I want to make love with you. I need to make love with you. In a few months I won't be very desirable, and I want to be loved by you while I still can. Don't you understand? I need this!"

"Oh, Honey, I'm sorry. You are the most desirable woman I've ever met, and I'll still desire you in two months, six months, forever and ever."

"Austin, I'm not dead yet and I want you to stop acting like I am." Maddie shifted her body and pulled out of her lover's arms.

"I'm concerned for you!" Austin knew she was only making excuses. If she were being honest, she didn't know how to act. She was angry and terrified at the same time.

Maddie cupped her face and said, "Sweetheart, I know you're upset and scared. So am I. I don't want to die and leave you. I pictured us growing old together. Sitting on the porch swing, drinking tea and talking about our lives, but God has other plans for me and you. I don't want you to mope around and not live your life when I'm gone. I want you to be happy and find love again."

"No way, Maddie! You're it for me. I'm not going to find anyone else. I promise I'll be happy, but I can't promise I'll find love again. Please don't ask me to." The tears were rolling down her face as she looked at her beautiful partner.

"Baby, please don't say that. I've seen how your Daddy lives. I don't want a life without love for you. I don't want you to be alone. Please say you won't do the same thing your Dad did." Maddie was crying as well.

"We're a fine pair. It's going to be hard to make love if we're both drowning in tears." Maddie laughed at Austin's joke and pulled her close.

"I love you so much. Please make love to me." Austin looked into Maddie's eyes and knew she would do whatever she wanted for as long as she wanted. They had made slow, tender love and when they were done, Austin kissed Maddie lightly all over her face and body. Soon after, Maddie fell asleep and her lover knew time was not on their side. This simple act of love would be the last time she would be able to be intimate with the woman she cherished with every breath she took.

Buckston was in the room with Austin the day Maddie died. He had been by her side every day, the moment the hospice nurse had said it wouldn't be long. Austin heard a sniffle behind her and knew he was trying to hold back his tears. Anguished, Austin felt her heart break with each gasp Maddie made. *I don't know how I am going to face this life alone. What am I going to do without her?* She looked at her father, begging him to fix this mess. After a few minutes, she heard a final gasp and knew she wouldn't hear another one. Her lover's physical body had died.

The nurse came into the bedroom when Buckston called for him, checked Maddie's vital signs and said, "She's gone. I'm so sorry for your loss." Austin continued to hold her lover's hand, stroking her thumb across the pad of the deceased woman's hand.

"I'll go make the necessary calls," the nurse said as he left the room.

Buckston squeezed her shoulder and walked out of the room as well. Austin looked at her love, knowing this would be the last time she saw her. Her lover looked so peaceful, her pain and suffering finally over. Austin stood up and let go of Maddie's hand, ran her fingers through the dead woman's hair one more time and then kissed her forehead. She walked out of the room to a life she never expected to live alone.

~~~~~

Several months had passed since Maddie had died. The funeral had been a celebration of Maddie's life. She had left strict instructions indicating those who attended had to have a good time with lively music, and only tell funny stories. All of Maddie's friends and family had attended. They had stopped coming around after hospice started coming to the house. It had been too difficult to see the woman they had loved and so full of life succumb to the awful disease.

Austin had tried to do what Maddie wanted, but had failed. She kept up a good front for everyone but when she went home at night she curled up in their bed and cried herself to sleep. Maddie wanted her love to remember all the good times they shared, not the last year of her life.

The middle of the night was the worst time for the dreams. Austin struggled with sleeping because she knew the dreams would come. The dream always started the same way. The sun was beating down on her as she mowed the lawn. Maddie was sitting on the porch swing, reading a book and sipping lemonade. Her favorite place to be, especially in the summer, when Austin was working in the yard. They had bought the house because of the front porch and big yard surrounding the house. When they had moved into the house, Austin had surprised her love with the porch swing.

Maddie had mentioned when they began dating that her dream was to live in a two-story home with a veranda running the length of the house and an acre of land surrounding the house. She had wanted two or three kids, but she was unable to have children. They had waited until Maddie was in her late thirties but discovered she wouldn't be able to carry a baby to term. Austin was older, so they had contented themselves with spoiling their nephews.

Autin finished her work and drove the mower back into the shed. She made her way up the steps and was about to lean down and kiss her partner when Maddie looked up, "I love you so much. I can't imagine my life without you. I love our life together. I want us to die old together peacefully in our sleep."

"Oh darlin', I love the idea of us growin' old together." She leaned down and slowly kissed Maddie, running her tongue lightly across her lips.

Maddie raised her arms and wrapped them around her partner's neck, pulling her lover into her lap. They both laughed as the swing moved back and forth. Austin leaned in, starting a kissing session that seemed to go on for hours, but was only a few minutes. As they kissed, Austin was touching Maddie all over her body, loving her with her lips and hands.

Austin began to undo Maddie's blouse, but her lover touched her hand and stopped her. "No, we can't, not here. The neighbors might see, let's go in." Maddie got up and walked toward the door. She was never one for personal displays of affection out in the open.

"I'll meet you in our room, wash up a bit before you come in." Austin watched her backside sway as she walked into the house. Her lover's butt drove her crazy with desire. Touching and rubbing Maddie's butt sent shivers down her spine as did the anticipation of the act.

Austin jumped up and made her way into the kitchen. The kitchen had a big ceramic farmhouse sink and was one of her favorite places to wash up. She could stand at the sink for minutes at a time and look at the backyard in bloom. She would watch the bees migrate from one flower to the next, pollinating the flowers. Watching the birds jump from the bird feeder to the bird bath, singing and splashing as they moved around the yard, made her laugh.

Maddie would always make sure the feeders were full every morning ensuring the birds didn't go hungry. Austin would laugh and kiss her, teasing the woman she loved saying, "The birds aren't going to go hungry if you miss one feeding." Maddie would slap her arm and tell her they might, and it was her duty as a lover of nature to make sure the birds were taken care of on a day-to-day basis. Besides, when she left this world, she hoped she could come back as bird. She wanted to fly and sweep through the trees just like the birds.

As Austin looked out the window, she washed her hands and face. She used the kitchen towel to wipe her arms down. The air from the air conditioner felt good after being outside. She could feel goosebumps all over her body and the tiny pebbles weren't only from the cool interior of the house. She was turned on and wanted Maddie so much. Austin made her way out of the kitchen and up the stairs to their bedroom. When she pushed the door open, the room was empty. The luscious bed looked inviting but was empty. She looked down the hall toward the bathroom and yelled, "Maddie, are you in there? Maddie?" She paused listening for her lover's sweet voice. "Maddie, where are you?"

She moved through every room in the house and couldn't find Maddie. *Maybe she went out front, thinking I was still outside.* Austin went to the front porch and when she didn't find her, she went down the front steps and around to the backyard searching for her partner.

"Maddie, where are you? Stop teasing me, where are you?" She was beginning to get upset. There was no sign of her partner. She continued to look for her, calling her name, begging her not to be gone.

"Maddie? Maddie? No ... no ... no don't be gone. Please, don't leave me." She yelled and dropped to the ground encircling her body with her arms and rocking back and forth, repeating "No, no, no, no don't leave me again." Austin always woke with a start, searching with her eyes and her heart, but never finding her love. *Dammit, another dream.* She felt the tears rolling down the sides of her cheeks. *Oh, Maddie, why did you leave me?* She continued to cry throughout the night and for many more nights.

FINAL GOODBYE

On the three-year anniversary of Maddie's death, Austin stood by her grave with her Father. The gravestone was medium-sized, with an image of a mockingbird, Maddie's favorite bird. The memorial read: **Madelaine Suzanne Williams – Loving partner and friend – May the birds in heaven let her fly**. Austin put a yellow rose in the flower holder and stepped back from the grave.

"Daddy, I don't know what I'm going to do. I feel as if I'm in a lake of quicksand. The harder I try to get out of it, the deeper I sink."

"I know darlin'. These last three years have not been easy for any of us. Your brothers and I have been watching you fade away with each passing day. You need to make a change in your life. Staying in that house all alone where there are constant reminders of Maddie is not good for you." He put his arm around her and hugged her closer to him.

Austin shrugged, "Dallas and Junior have said the same thing to me. I know I need to do something, but I can't make up my mind what I want to do. I'm so frustrated. It's as if all my decision-making power died with Maddie." Tears streaked down her face, dripping onto her shirt. Her days seemed to be filled with her crying or being depressed to the point where she didn't want to get out of bed, even after three years. She was tired of feeling like she was existing and not living. She rubbed her eyes and buried her face in her Father's neck.

He was a couple of inches taller and her head fit perfectly. She breathed in the scent of his Stetson cologne and the muskiness of horses. This was always a comfort to her. Austin looked like her Father. They were both tall and willowy. They had piercing blue eyes. Ice-cold one minute and warm as a summer sky the next. Their reddish-brown skin tone made them look like they were tan all the time, even in the middle of winter. Both had white hair and kept it buzzed close to their heads.

When people asked why she kept her hair cut so short, she would say jokingly "I'm not defined by my hair." She had started shaving her head when Maddie lost her hair and found she liked the cut. Her hair was easy to take care of and she could wet her head on hot summer days to cool off.

Buckston squeezed her and said, "Your brothers are right, you need to do something, but I know you can't seem to make the move. Don't get mad, but we have a suggestion for you." She raised her head and looked at him. He could tell she was preparing to tell him no, but he beat her to the punch.

"Now, don't say no, before you hear me out. I remembered how much you and your brothers loved going camping when you were kids and I was thinking that might be what you need."

"Dad, I'm not going to go pitch a tent somewhere and meditate my way out of my grief." Austin was beginning to shake her head no.

"No, of course not, we wouldn't even consider a tent, we thought maybe you might like an RV instead." He looked at her, hoping she would hear him out. She looked at him incredulously.

"A recreational vehicle, why on earth would you think an RV would be the answer? I mean, what would I do? I have mine and Maddie's home and you need me. I have my job with our landscaping company. I can't just pick up and go camping."

"Sweetheart, you can sell your home. You can retire from the job. Make a fresh start. Your brothers are here if I need anything. You need to get away and if you decide you want to come back home, you can sell the RV and buy another house. Think of it as a vacation." He looked at her with loving eyes trying to infuse into her the adventurous spirit she once had before Maddie died.

"You think this is best. I mean, I don't know. Selling the home Maddie and I bought together and leaving you. It's going to be hard. I just don't know." He knew he had her. His heart did a happy dance.

"It's okay, baby doll. I know this is going to be good for you. Your brothers and I will get you all set up and you know, Nancy can sell the house for you. Dallas has already talked to her about the sale and she thinks she can get you top dollar for the house. With the money from the sale and your retirement you'll get from the company, you should be fine going out on the road for a while." Nancy was the number one real-estate broker in the county and since she was married to Austin's brother Dallas, the thought of selling her house was less stressful. Buckston held her tighter and kissed the top of her head.

"Well, what about safety? Aren't you worried something might happen to me out on the road by myself?" It was a last-ditch attempt to talk herself out of this idea more than it was to talk her Dad out of it.

"Austin Lee Stevens don't try to kid a kidder. You're one of the toughest gals I know so N-O, I am not afraid for you." He grinned at her and she laughed.

"Okay, well then you best show me what you had in mind. I've got a lot of planning to do if I'm going to be leaving soon." She looked down at the grave of her dead partner, feeling a bit better about her future. She was still going to miss Maddie like crazy, but a change of scenery would not be a bad thing.

Austin had gone shopping with her brothers and her Dad looking at RV's and found the perfect rig for her travels. The recreational vehicle was a used 32-foot Fleetwood Jamboree. She especially loved the interior because instead of having cabinets and seating along both sides of the vehicle, the layout was open on one side with a bank of windows. The RV was bright and cheery on the inside and the décor was simple. The motorized home was what she needed to start the next adventure in her life.

Plus, with her Father's negotiating skills, she paid a good price and had money left over to buy herself a used Jeep Grand Cherokee. She would need a vehicle to get around and since the Jeep already had a front tow package installed, she thought she would try it out. Austin was going to need a vehicle to drive around, once she parked the rig at the RV park. She fell in love with the vehicle as soon as she took the SUV for a drive. The color was silver with a light leather interior. The Jeep had a V8 engine and she loved the idea of extra power especially on mountain roads. The vehicle was a tough girl's luxury machine, which is how Junior described her when she drove over to show her family.

She spent a few weeks making the RV her own. She had a love seat removed and added a rocker recliner. The kitchen and bathroom were modernized with backsplash. All the carpet was replaced. Austin shook her head when she saw the original beige carpet, astounded at the idea that light-colored carpet was good for camping and muddy campsites. She chose hard-wood looking linoleum with the idea of adding a few rugs to add more warmth to the interior. The finished product looked like a brand-new home on wheels.

Two months after her conversation with her Father at Maddie's grave, she was ready to head out on her adventure. She had mapped out everywhere she wanted to go over the next year or so and promised to call her Dad and brothers as much as she could, which ended up being almost every night for the first year. She struggled with being by herself, but the change in scenery helped to bring her out of her funk and at least, help her feel like she was living.

~~~~~

Five years had passed since Maddie passed away and Austin decided the time was right to settle down but going back home wasn't appealing. She had spent a lot of time grieving and Maddie would have been disgusted, because she had spent so much time wallowing in her pain. After she bought the RV and had been on the road for a year, she had adopted Clara Jane, a miniature Doberman pincher/chihuahua mix and Rocky Bob, a Jack Russell terrier mix.

After traveling around the country, she was ready to settle down in one place for a while. Although she had thought about returning to her hometown in Texas, she decided she still wasn't ready to move back home. She needed more time and so she had talked to some of her fellow travelers and found out about the Park Attendant jobs that came up on a regular basis at parks all over the United States. Her friend Gus Sparrow had told her about a job in Arizona. She applied and got the job.

When she had worked for her family, most of her time has been spent outdoors working in people's gardens and yards. An RV Park Attendant role helped her stay in shape and she liked doing manual labor. The job also allowed her to use her landscaping skills, which she missed. There was something to be said about getting your hands dirty in the soil. She felt working in the dirt was a spiritual experience.

The drive had been a long one. Leaving her home state of Texas to travel to Arizona and work as an RV Park Attendant had sounded like a good idea two months ago. "I know of a Park Attendant job and you have enough experience," her friend Gus said. "I've got just the place for you, outside of Flagstaff. The park is called the Purple Cactus RV Park and the attendant left due to family illness. They need someone right away."

She had been in Amarillo at a RV park working as a temporary attendant. She found she enjoyed working at the parks helping where she could. At fifty-five, she knew she needed to find ways to stay in shape. Working out wasn't something she enjoyed, but she did like working with her hands and being outdoors.

"Okay guys, we're here" Austin said as she maneuvered the Jamboree into the Purple Cactus RV Park parking lot. She heard two quiet whines from the confines of the traveling home. She looked back in the direction of the whines and saw two little heads with ears standing straight up, tails wagging, tongues lolling.

Austin smiled, "What ya think Clara Jane, are you ready to get out of your bed? I know, I know, you guys have been cooped up for the last two hours. Rocky Bob, don't you growl at me, you know being in your bed is part of the drill." She reached back and opened the kennel for the two animals.

"Okay, my little pumpernickels, let's check things out." She clipped a leash to each of her dog's harnesses and opened the door.

She had arrived in early afternoon and the weather was warm but not too hot. There was a slight breeze and she could smell the campfires scattered throughout the park. When she decided to work in an RV park on a full-time basis, she had looked at several she had visited on her travels, but Gus' recommendation of the park in Arizona seemed to fit the bill for her, plus they needed someone right away and with Gus as a reference, she didn't have a difficult time getting the job.

She looked around the park. The grounds had plenty of shade trees, a small store and a big fenced-in dog run. The run had to be at least an acre and she knew the dogs would love being able to stretch their legs and run in the open space. A bonus was she would get to mow the grass. Mowing was one of her favorite ways to unwind. She used to mow her yard all the time and took great pleasure in creating the lines in the grass when she ran the mower up and down. She knew the sense of pride was silly but there was something about the lines that made her feel as if she had done a good job.

Each campsite had a small concrete pad with a newly renovated picnic table and an open area with a fire pit ring in the center. She could see stacks of wood up by the office and she knew one of the perks of working at the park was free firewood. She loved to make a fire and stare into the flames for hours at a time. Sometimes watching was relaxing and sometimes the act would bring back memories of Maddie. Either way, she loved to stoke the flames and watch the wood crumble to ashes.

The park backed up to a river and the owner had explained that one of her duties was to keep the grass down. Rattlesnakes loved to hide in the tall grass and since the walking paths followed the river, keeping the grass down would eliminate anyone getting bit by the pesky reptiles. She could already see she had her work cut out for her. The grass was high and there was no doubt the growth was because of all the rain the region had been receiving over the summer months.

The park amenities were amazing. They had a laundry, swimming pool, and a dog wash, which she was looking forward to using. Washing dogs in the little camper sink was not easy even if the dogs were small. The park was located near Flagstaff, which meant she was close to a city. The temperature was moderate in the summer, which she wanted. Austin figured if she was going to take up this kind of work then the park had to have everything. She would want her provisional home to be as comfortable as possible for her and the dogs.

As she looked around, she heard a door slam, then a voice. "You must be Austin Stevens, I'm so excited to meet you!" Austin turned and watched as a man, who appeared to be in his sixties or maybe seventies made his way toward her.

He had a long stride and his age didn't seem to be hindering him in any way. He was as tall as she and had thick mane of white hair covered by a sweat-stained Stetson. He wore working man's attire -- blue jeans and a work shirt with gloves sticking out of his back pocket. His boots were worn down and looked like they had seen better days. He was in front of her before she could blink an eye and had his hand stuck out in greeting. She shifted one of the leashes to her left hand and reached out to shake his hand.

"I'm Barney Wilton." His hands were callused and swallowed her hand as they shook.

"Barney, so nice to meet ya," Austin said as she shifted the leashes back into her right hand. "I believe we spoke on the phone. Gus spoke very highly of you."

"Yeah, Gus and I go way back. I've been watching for you." The old man said as he glanced over her shoulder at the parked RV. "Nice rig."

"Thanks! She's done some travelin' over the last two years, but I think we're ready to settle down for a while. I know I am. I can't tell you how much I appreciate your meeting me like this. Rudy Wellman told me you looked after the place when he was gone." She continued to look around as she spoke.

Out of the corner of her eye, Austin saw a woman walking around an area that appeared to be set aside for a business. She wasn't sure what it was supposed to be, but she was intrigued by the woman. Wow, *she is cute,* Austin thought absentmindedly as she refocused her attention on Barney.

"Yeah Rudy and I go way back. We both started our businesses at the same time and have always looked after each other. Since he's going to be gone for a few months, all you need to do is give me a call and I'll come running. I'm down the road a couple of miles." He said pointing down the road. "I live on a few acres with my dog and horses. I run a horseback riding business so if people ask for things to do, you can send them my way. For example, Jane Langston, the office manager, usually sends people my way. You'll meet her later." He gestured toward the office.

"Sure thing, Barney, I've spoken a few times to Mrs. Langston on the phone and I'll be happy to send people your way, if Ms. Langston doesn't get to them first." She winked and glanced back over to the intriguing woman who had her back turned to Austin.

She has the cutest bubble butt, I've ever seen. Wait, what? Good Lord, Austin, what are you thinking? You're a broken-down widow, who still cries herself to sleep every night over a partner she lost five years ago. Oh, well, nothing wrong with lookin'.

She nodded toward the woman. "Say, Barney? What's going on over there?" The petite blonde had caught her eye again, and Austin was mesmerized by the smile directed toward her customers. In her mind, she equated the wattage to a bright light shining from a lighthouse, showing her soul the way home.

"Oh, that's Jaime Crocket's place. She set up a bookshop for the guests, oh . . ." he scratched his head and looked in the direction Austin indicated . . . "I'd say about a year or so ago. The shop's been a real hit and because people liked the idea, she managed to stay on with the park."

The bookshop was in a great location, the center of park, which was to the left of the main office. *Hmm...prime real estate for a business like hers*, Austin thought as she watched the woman work. "It looks as if she loves what she's doing."

"Oh, yes, she does. Everyone who stays at the park loves her. I bet half the people who came back this year came back because of her. She has a great sense of humor and a sparkling personality. I really like her. She brings me dinner once a week and let me tell you, she plays a mean hand of gin rummy." Barney laughed as he started walking toward a parked ATV.

"Hmm ... thanks for filling me in on the goings-on of the park," Austin said as she looked down at her dogs, Clara Jane and Rocky Bob. They looked back at her with tongues lolling, waiting for her to take them for a walk. "All right, you guys let's go get our rig moved so we can get camp set up."

The rancher reached the ATV and said, "Let's get you settled. I'll give you the grand tour once you've settled in. I've got you in a reserved spot for full-time park people. The campsite is over this way in a little grove of trees by the stream. I think you're going to like your new home. The site is a bit out of the way to give you privacy, but not too far that you can't keep up with everything going on in the park."

"Great, thanks Barney." Austin watched him as he hopped on a modified utility ATV. She marveled at his flexibility and agility. Her Dad was about the same age as Barney and he could barely get around, because he broke his back twice in his younger, rodeo days. She was glad her brothers were taking care of him, because she would have felt guilty in taking this job and not moving back home. Their support of her and their Father had made the move possible. She put the dogs in the RV and walked around to the driver's side and started the RV. As Barney took off down the road, she put the vehicle in drive and followed him.

TALL DRINK OF WATER

"O-M-G, who is the tall drink of water?" Oscar Olivas exclaimed as he watched the woman who had pulled into the park a few minutes earlier.

Jaime turned from pouring him a glass of wine to see who he was talking about. "For a gay guy, you sure seem to notice women," Jaime admonished him, thinking, *Wow! He is right, she is one fine drink of ... hmmm ... not water, something stronger I think, maybe whiskey. Ohhhhh yeaaaah! A perfect description for an Amazon. Yummy!*

"I'm looking out for you James. I think you should get back out there. You've been single way too long and I know you want someone in your life. It's been over three years since you and Angie broke up. Besides Titus needs another Mommy, don't ya think?" He lifted the glass of wine and took a sip.

Jaime was only half listening. "Yes, you're right" she said absentmindedly.

Her attention was focused on the woman standing on the road. The woman was gorgeous and quirky at the same time. She had on a straw cowboy hat and wore a blue tank top that framed out firm, muscular arms and small, perky breasts. The woman wore cut-off jean shorts to the knees, surrounding shapely, long legs tucked into bright red cowboy boots. Jaime grinned at the look, realizing the woman had pulled it off. Jaime was practically drooling, and she knew right away that she was going to have to get to know the Amazonian slash heart-stopping cowgirl woman, for sure.

The Amazon was tall, at least six feet if not taller. The cowboy hat was pushed up so Jaime could see her face. Tanned with a few freckles and the bluest eyes Jaime had ever seen. The tank top helped to accentuate her sky colored eyes. The petite blonde couldn't tell what the woman's hair looked like as her mane was hidden from sight by the hat. There wasn't anything sticking out from under the hat so her hair couldn't be very long. The moment made Jaime feel as if she heard her thoughts because the Amazon took her hat off to scratch her head. She was practically bald. Her hair was cut short, shaved-off and the color was gray -- almost white in the sun. Her head was the perfect shape for the cut and she pulled it off. Jaime was drawn to her look immediately.

As she turned her gaze to the woman's arms, her first assessment was not wrong, the arms were muscular, but not overly so. Jaime figured she was one of those people who worked out or was blessed with the perfect shape. Her butt wasn't too big, but the bump was big enough to be shaped like a small bubble. The small woman could see herself running her hands up and down those tight buns. She shivered as she thought about other places, she would like to run her hands. The woman was wearing a big silver bracelet on her left wrist with a matching ring. The stone looked to be turquoise, but the distance between them made identifying the stone difficult.

Jaime loved the way the woman looked, giving her a sense of power without having to exert much energy. She had never been attracted to women who looked butch or androgynous, but as she gazed at this woman, she thought she might have to rethink her thoughts because she was attracted to her. She wanted to get to know her. The woman didn't seem to notice Jaime, but Jaime sure noticed her. She was like a Popsicle on a hot summer day and the bookshop owner wanted to cool herself off with a few licks.

Jaime wanted to go up to her and smell and taste her. *What am I thinking? I never act this way about a woman.* As she watched her talk to Barney, the Amazon smiled, and Jaime's heart skipped a beat. She had two dimples and her smile would light up the night. She had the whitest teeth Jaime had ever seen. The woman kept getting better and better. *I have got to get to know her. Now, all I need to do is figure out how I can meet her without being obvious,* Jaime thought as she turned her attention to her bookshop and Oscar.

Jaime lifted her wine glass in salute to Oscar and he gave her a wink. "I am definitely going to need to get to know her and introduce Titus to her," she said as she took a long swallow of her Pinot Grigio. "How old do you think she is?"

"Oh, I'd say she's around our age, but I can't tell at this distance." He glanced at the woman again to see if he could figure out her age. "Her hair, what little there is, shouts she might be a tad bit older than us. Hmm ... I'm intrigued," Oscar said as he watched her follow Barney to his ATV. Their conversation lasted a few more moments and then she got into her RV. The behemoth headed off down the road and Jaime was excited because she could see the Amazon's RV was going to be parked close to hers.

"Looks as if she is getting the prime spot next to you in the little grove of trees," Oscar commented as he took a sip from his wine glass and watched Jaime out of the corner of his eye. He was her best friend and had been for many years. His dark looks complemented her lightness and when people saw them together, they commented on how they looked like the yin-yang of human beings. Little did they know how accurate they were about their friendship. Oscar was the yang to her yin.

When most people looked at Oscar, they thought he looked like a god. He had a strong jaw with an aquiline nose, which he thought was a flaw, but Jaime assured him his nose gave him character. He had jet-black hair that sometimes looked blue in the right light. His eyes were milk-chocolate brown and there had been many women who said they could drown in his eyes, until they found out he was gay. Shaking their heads, they would say what a shame, womankind's loss.

He could tell Jaime was intrigued and was jumping for joy on the inside. He had not seen his friend this interested in a woman since the Angie-capade, as he referred to the break-up. "She sure is good-looking. Are you going to use your womanly wiles to get to know her?" he teased as he took another sip of his wine.

"I don't know, maybe. Since she's working at the park, I'll have the opportunity. Barney told me she was coming today. Although, she may have a partner or husband." Jaime kept her gaze on the spot where the Amazon had been standing long after she and her dogs had left.

"Hello, are you in there? Jaime to earth!"

She re-focused her attention on him. "Yes, I'm here! Stop bothering me, I've got work to do." The shopkeeper gave Oscar a slight smirk and walked over to the kid's area inside the small trailer she called The Reading Nook. There were books to be rearranged.

Some children had come in earlier and pulled out a bunch of the books and left them stacked everywhere. She didn't mind having to pick up after them. The housekeeping gave her a chance to think about the new woman in the park and she definitely wanted to think about the woman. The Amazon was gorgeous as far as Jaime was concerned. Being almost fifty, the bookshop owner felt her choice of beautiful women was limited.

Most women she had met were either way too butch in appearance or too controlling in their mannerisms. She wasn't interested in either type. Unfortunately, in her experience those types of women were the only women available in the small city of Flagstaff.

She appreciated Oscar's efforts when he tried to fix her up, but his idea of a good date was an expensive meal and lots of sex. Not her cup of tea, she wanted to get to know someone. She was old enough to know that you don't find a viable partner by having sex with them on the first date. She wasn't a total prude and she had had sex on a first date, but those women were not dating material -- just satisfying-a-need-material.

Jaime walked around her little square plot thinking about how she got to this point in her life. When she had retired from her software job, she decided she was going to travel the country and make money by investing in a traveling bookshop. The first couple of years, she wandered all over the United States, stopping in different towns for a month at a time, operating her bookshop/coffee/wine shop. She received lots of attention and the permanent RV'ers seemed to love the idea of having a cup of coffee or glass of wine while searching for the next book they wanted to read.

She enjoyed interacting with the different people, but she got tired of driving all over the place and wanted to find somewhere she could call home. She had been to the Purple Cactus several times in her travels and absolutely loved the park. She struck up a deal with Rudy Wellman, the park owner, to get a permanent space for her RV and the bookshop. She wasn't getting rich, but she had enough to pay for her spot and have a little extra to supplement her retirement.

As she tidied up the books, she wondered what the woman sounded like when she spoke and what she smelled like. *Did she wear perfume?* No, Jaime figured she didn't. *I bet she has a husky voice, one that when she speaks, sends tingles down the spine. Yum!* She thought as she absentmindedly cleaned off tables.

"Hey, girlie, are you still daydreaming about the tall drink of water?" Oscar asked as he made his way into the trailer to stand beside her.

"Good gosh, Oscar, don't walk up on a girl deep in thought. You scared the crap out of me." He had startled her out of her reverie, and she did not appreciate the interruption. Oscar finished his drink and reminded her of their dinner plans the following evening. She waved him off and began gathering up her tables and chairs to lock inside the trailer for another night. She finished out her routine by balancing out the cash register and gathering up her money bag with the day's receipts.

Her cat Titus, a giant male, showed up rubbing on her legs as she made her way down the path to her little home. "Titus, you rascal, stop trying to trip me. Where have you been?" He looked at her as if to say, "That's for me to know and you to find out."

"Don't look at me that way, buddy. I know you've got a girlfriend on the other side of the park. I better not get a note saying you knocked her up." She picked him up before he tripped her, snuggling into his sweet face. He was almost as big as she was but her small stature didn't prohibit her from carrying him around like a baby. She gave him loving kisses as she cooed and told him what a wonderful little cat he was and how much she loved him.

~~~~~

Austin turned the RV onto the road as she followed Barney. He drove past three spots and stopped by one nestled in a copse of trees. She could easily back her rig into the spot and have her camp set up in no time. She stepped out of her home on wheels and walked over his idling ATV.

"Do you need help backing in?" the old man asked as he stood and lifted his leg to get off the ATV.

"Nah, I'm good. I've backed in many times by myself," She said, waving her hand indicating he should stay on the four-wheeler.

"Okay, well don't hesitate to call if you need me. I gave ya my number, didn't I?" He patted his shirt pocket, looking for his cell phone.

"Yes, sure did. I've got your number in my phone and sure appreciate all your help this afternoon." Austin smiled as she held up her phone.

"No problem, happy to help. I better get back to the ranch. I've got to prepare for a trip out early in the morning. See ya later." Barney revved the engine and waved as he drove off.

Austin enjoyed talking to the rancher. He was funny and had given her the low-down on the park and how everything worked. As she thought about their conversation, she conjured up the image of the woman running the bookstore. She was cute, no ifs ands or buts about it. The younger woman wore her hair in a short bob and appeared to be blonde with darker white streaks. Austin guessed the small woman to be about 5'4" and figured she didn't weigh much more than 100 pounds.

She'd had on lime-green crops with a peach-colored sleeveless blouse. Perfect for the warm summer day. To complete the casual, but classic look, the petite blonde was wearing flip-flops and had an air of elegance about her, making her casual attire look good, but not over-dressed for the park.

Austin got back in the RV and backed her rig into position. She had left plenty of room to let both her slide-outs out, one on each side, and there was shade on both sides from all the trees. "Oh! This will be nice when the weather warms up. We'll be cool all summer long," she said to the dogs as she got out of the mobile home to begin setting up camp.

The ground was level, which meant she didn't have to worry about leveling the RV. She hooked up the water, electric, and sewer line, not her favorite job, but the tasks had to be done. One of the reasons for a Class C RV was that a person could get the amenities found in a permanent home: water, electric, and sewer.

Austin spent a few minutes pulling out her camp chairs and placed them around the fire pit on the side where her main door opened and closed. She placed a tablecloth on the table to protect the paint job from getting scratched. She set her grill and cook top on one end of the bright blue picnic table, which was standard for all the sites. This area was perfect for her morning self-care regime where she spent time writing in her journal. She continued getting items out to make her campsite a home and finally got to the final task.

The button for the automatic awning was inside the door, and she was glad she had invested in it. The RV had come with a manual awning, but having her forearm pinched in the arm-extending mechanism as she was trying to set up the cover was the last straw for her. She had been bruised for weeks and still had a round, discolored scar on her arm.

Once the awning was out, she laid down an outdoor carpet and set up a pen for the dogs so they could be outside with her. She could have let them loose and they would have stayed close to her, but until she found out about the wildlife situation, she didn't want them to run free. She had read about the dangers of wildlife predators when she had looked over the website, and both Mr. Wellman and Barney had warned her about the packs of javelinas over the countryside. With the stream so close, she knew the park would be a prime spot for wild animals to come get drinks of water.

She brought the dogs out of the RV and put them in their pen. Both dogs looked up at her, waiting for her to put their beds in the pen as well. "Okay, give me a second, I'll get your beds set up. You've got carpet to lay on, so I don't know what the big deal is with having to have a bed, too."

She opened one of the side cubbies and pulled out two dog beds. Each one had a dog's name embroidered on the outside rim and when she put them in the pen, Clara Jane went to the one with Rocky Bob's name and Rocky Bob went to the one with Clara Jane's. "Crazy dogs, you don't even know how to spell." They looked at her as if to say, "You don't know what you are talking about. We know what we are doing." She laughed and took a Modelo Especial out of her cooler. She sat down in her rocking camp chair and contemplated meeting the blonde woman down the road.

The sun was low in the sky reflecting orange, pink and purple highlights when Austin roused herself from the chair and went inside to start getting dinner ready. She was going to celebrate her first night with her favorite meal -- filet mignon, baked potato and watermelon. She brought food out for the dogs and went over to the fire pit to start a fire.

"Nothing like sitting by the fire as you eat dinner," she mumbled to herself as she put the Firestarter log and the pinion wood into the pit. She lit the log and watched the flames start eating away at the wood. Once the fire was burning, she turned on the grill and started to make her meal. She was looking forward to a quiet evening, eating a good meal, and reading one of the books she had stored on her Kindle.

Although, Austin thought she might be persuaded to switch to a real book if buying a paperback meant she could get to know the bookshop owner. She loved her Kindle and was always downloading books, usually sequels to one of her favorite author's stories. The fact that Kindle showed the reader the next book in line had not been lost on her. She marveled at their marketing techniques and she knew she was one of the bibliophiles who fell for their marketing ploys.

Living in an RV did not lend itself to collecting books and creating a library, but maybe she could make room for a few books. Also, the Wi-Fi was sketchy in most RV parks so being able to download a book wasn't always possible. She had heard that the bookshop had good Wi-Fi so another reason to go visit the bookshop. Austin tapped herself on the head as if an amazing idea came to fruition making up her mind that she wanted to visit the bookshop soon. *Maybe once I get settled into my job, I'll make time to visit. Sure, would be nice to get to know that little gal.* She looked in the direction of the bookshop, wondering what time the store opened and closed.

~~~~~

The Reading Nook bookshop was in a prime spot for everyone in the park. The park owner knew what he was doing when he offered to let Jaime have one of the spots near the office for her bookshop. Everyone in the park had to walk past the shop and most of them stopped to peruse her inventory of books. The towable she used for her bookshop had been outfitted as a horse trailer. She had painted the outside orange with blue lettering, advertising the name of her shop. She had the front of the trailer walled off for storage and the rest had floor-to-ceiling bookshelves with bars in the middle to keep the books from falling out when she pulled the trailer. She also had mobile bookcases that could be pushed up against the other bookcases and secured in place.

In front of the storage wall was her counter, housing her iPad, which was connected to her mobile Wi-Fi. She knew if she wanted to stand out in the park, besides selling books she had to make the internet available to her patrons. She had been frustrated too many times at other RV parks, trying to connect to the internet and not being able to, all because of spotty Wi-Fi connections. The money drawer for sales was housed under the counter along with a wine refrigerator.

The coffee machine that made everything from regular coffee to expresso was sitting on top of the counter. She had invested quite a bit of money in the machine, but the investment was worth the effort, as she could cater to the neophyte coffee drinker or to the haughty coffee drinker. Her wine inventory also met an expansive criterion and she was set to provide her customers with whatever they wanted in literary or beverage entertainment.

The back gates had been changed to a single automatic gate with the ability to close with a push of the button like a garage door. There was enough clearance for the door to be stored in the ceiling without impinging on customers who were tall. When the gate was up, she put down outdoor carpet where she placed a couple of bistro tables and chairs. There was also room for three outdoor club chairs designed for customers who wanted to linger reading their purchased book and drinking their chosen beverage. The bistro table and chairs were stackable for easy storage and the club chairs had rollers for movability. She had also installed an awning on the back end, so the chairs and tables were protected from the elements. The bookshop owner could easily lock everything down when she was on the move.

THE SHOP KEEPER

A few days had gone by since Austin had pulled into the park and she had been busy getting to know the park and learning her duties from Jane. Jaime had not seen much of the Amazon but knew what she was doing because she would check in with Jane, who was happy to share the latest goings-on at the park. Jane was a gossip and Jaime usually took everything she said with a grain of salt, but her interest in Austin had her visiting with Jane more often than she usually did.

"Hey, Jane, how are you today?"

"Well, I'll be. This is the most I've seen you in the office in I don't know, ever." Jane smirked at Jaime, knowing why she was there.

"What do you mean? I come by the office all the time." Jaime protested weakly.

"No, you don't. You've only started coming around since we got the handsome worker-bee."

"I have not. I thought I would check in with you is all. What's wrong with checking in?"

"Oh, there's nothing wrong with checking in, but I know you're more interested in checking in on Austin than you are in checking in with me." Jane chuckled as she teased Jaime.

Jaime knew she had been caught. "Okay, you got me there. I'm sorry."

"No need to be sorry. If I was a mind and a few years younger, I might give you a run for your money."

"Uh, what about your husband?"

"Oh, well, I knew there was another reason." Jane winked at Jaime. "Now, git on out of here and git back to work."

"Yes, ma'am." Jaime laughed as she slammed the door heading back to her store.

Jaime usually stayed open until sundown but would sometimes close early if her shop was deserted for more than a couple of hours. As was her habit, she put everything away and pushed the button to close the rear gate of the trailer. She had left the side door open because of the screen door. This allowed for a breeze to flow through when the smaller windows at the top of the trailer were open. Once the back door closed, she closed out her register for the night. She moved around the shop looking for holes on the shelves, making a list of books requiring reordering and straightening out books that had been misplaced. The action of closing her shop was comforting to her.

Jaime loved books and were a comfort to her all her life. As she got older and had settled into one career, she started setting yearly reading goals. Each year she increased her goal and her library. Reading was her escape and she reveled in the things she learned, places she traveled in her mind and the different characters she got to know in her books. Her ability to immerse herself in the stories had been an ongoing argument with the women she dated. They would tell her something and she would say okay not even realizing she was replying to them. Then when they would ask if she did what they asked she would say she didn't know what they were talking about, which would cause an argument.

Jaime couldn't help her love of reading, but if she were honest no one had made enough of an impression on her to make her want to pay more attention. Her books were her best friends, her way to deal with life, and the one thing she could count on to always be there -- except for Oscar. He often teased her about the pecking order in her life: her books would be first, followed by Titus, her bookshop, her Subaru, her scooter, which she purchased to take short trips and save money on gas, and then him. She would laugh and tell him he was ahead of her scooter.

When she turned fifty, she realized she didn't want to waste any more time dreaming of seeing the places in her books -- she wanted to go to them in person. The bibliophile decided to take retirement early from her company and start traveling. She had invited Oscar to go with her, but he wasn't ready to wander around the world, so she kept him up to date with her travels through email and phone.

At first, she traveled to different parts of the world. She had invested very well during her years of working so she could afford to travel if she stayed within her budget. She also wanted to visit the wonders of the U.S., so after three years of world travel, she invested in a Teardrop towable. The trailer could be towed behind her Subaru and the vehicle combination allowed her to start her travel around the United States. She asked Oscar again to travel with her since she was back in the U.S., but he didn't want to upend his life. He liked his job and wanted to stay where he would have more access to dating men.

During her U.S. travels she had an epiphany: RV parks were missing a business opportunity. People who traveled in RV's or pulled towables were always looking for something to do in the evenings. The internet service was not dependable at most places, so watching movies or TV was a struggle. Reading was the one thing a person could do without having to rely on technology.

There were those people who only wanted to use technology such as the Kindle and most of the time those kinds of people who find an internet café in the nearest town to get the books they wanted to read. Jaime thought, Kindles were great, and she didn't have anything against them, but they did require extra work if there was no Wi-Fi available at the park.

Besides she felt there was something to be said for holding a book. The weight and smell of paper were comforting to her and she gambled that other people felt the same way. Her time at the Purple Cactus had proved her point. She found a small trailer she could convert and within a few months, she had her bookshop. Her life was almost perfect, but she did get lonely.

Jaime had dated and even had a few partners, but she had never found The One. She struggled with trust and before long the relationship would end usually because of her. Her partners wanted more than she could give and eventually they would grow apart. Her most recent partner, Amy, had lasted the longest -- three years. They had both been focused on their careers and settling down with partner and a family had not been in the cards for Jaime.

Amy had wanted to take their relationship to the next logical step, move in together and grow old, but Amy wasn't the one for Jaime and she couldn't see growing old with her. Jaime hadn't allowed Amy all the way into her heart. She didn't trust her enough to give her girlfriend her whole heart.

Growing up, she had learned that giving your heart away to people would eventually hurt, because they always let you down. She had enough pain in her young life, so she kept herself at a distance, never letting herself get too close to anyone except for Oscar. Amy had tolerated him, but Jaime knew she didn't like him. She was jealous of the one person Jaime let all the way in and she struggled at keeping the peace when those two were in the same room. If the bookshop owner were honest with herself, she was relieved when Amy pushed for more because the pressure gave Jaime the out, she needed to end the relationship.

She had met Oscar as a young person. The petite blonde had been cornered on the playground by one of the bullies in their school. She was prepared to take him on, but Oscar stepped in and defended her. Jaime had been irritated at his assuming she needed help, but he had reassured her. He knew she could have defended herself, but why mess up the bully's face when he could talk the bully down. He had literally saved her face and made her feel okay about him stepping in at the same time. They became inseparable and he always had her back. She trusted and loved him and no matter what, he was there by her side.

He had followed her to Flagstaff stating, "Lady love, you know I can't live without you any longer. Of course, I'm going to leave Phoenix and come up north with you. If nothing else, you need someone to keep an eye on you. You know how you always manage to get into trouble when I'm not around."

She had scoffed at him and he had grinned, both knowing the real reason he was following her. He loved her like a sister and didn't want to be too far away from her. He needed to be there to protect her and she loved him even more for his gesture. Once again, he had proved he was there to watch her back.

~~~~~

After Jaime closed the bookshop, she headed back to her RV, which was an upgrade from the towable Teardrop. She needed more space if she was going to stay in one park for a longer time. Her

RV was a class C and she described the interior of the vehicle as a shotgun model. A person entered through a side door and the kitchen was on one side which spanned the length of the RV to the bedroom and on the other side was the dinette and couch with recliners on both ends. The bedroom was in the back with the shower on the side of the kitchen and the toilet on the side of the dinette.

When a person walked into her home, they felt right at home. Her furniture was a light cream color and she had used brown accents to add further warmth. She loved the look and feel of her portable home. She had removed one small couch next to the entrance and put in a floor-to-ceiling bookcase that housed her most cherished books. Her favorite thing to do after a day at work was to come home, pour a glass of wine, and pick one of her books to read for a while. She had read all of them and it didn't matter to her where she started or ended, she loved reading her books.

Her arrival at the RV was met with a desperate meow. Titus was rubbing against her legs pushing so hard she almost fell. "Okay, buddy, stop trying to trip me. I'll let you out. You be careful. I don't want you to become owl or coyote food." She laughed to herself, as the cat was almost the size of a bobcat and the small predators steered clear of the feline. She opened the door and Titus took off into the night.

As she shut the door, she realized she couldn't get the woman who had arrived at the beginning of the week out of her mind. She contemplated how she was going to get to know this new addition to the park. "I could bake her some cookies and do the neighborly thing and take them over to her. I think I have everything I need." She began to pull out ingredients needed to make chocolate-chip cookies. "Everybody likes chocolate-chip cookies, right?" As she pulled a bowl out of a cabinet and started mixing ingredients for the batch.

At dusk, she was ready to take her cookies over to the new woman's place. She had arranged them on a nice sized paper plate covered in plastic wrap. The cat hadn't come back yet, but Jaime wasn't too worried. He was always out and about until bedtime. Jaime stepped out of her RV and began following the path to where the Amazon had her rig parked. She had become good friends with the last person who had lived there. Sarah Gardner had been the Park Attendant and Jaime missed her since she had to move away. "When family needs you, you go," Sarah had said.

You meet new people, get to know them, become friends and then they move on. Jaime was used to people moving in and out of her life. She had stayed in touch with her which was unusual. She enjoyed having a female friend but continued her standard way of acting with friends by keeping her at arm's length. Oscar had been the one constant she had allowed in her life, but deep down, in a moment of introspection, she wished she had more friends.

Her flashlight bobbed up and down on the path as she made her away through to the Amazon's RV. There were a few lights on the paths, but not many. The owner had wanted to allow the ambience of the woods to permeate the atmosphere of the park. As she approached the camp site she called out, "Yoo-hoo, okay to come in?"

"Sure, come on in." Jaime stepped into the light of the campsite and she could not believe her eyes. Titus was curled up in the woman's lap, purring and swishing his tail back and forth. A clear indicator he was content.

Austin had been surprised when the big cat showed up at her site. He looked at her and the two dogs, sauntered by the pen as if he owned the place and proceeded to jump up in her lap. He had been there ever since. She marveled at how heavy he was and how his body covered the whole length of her legs when he stretched out. He had maneuvered around trying to decide which was the most comfortable position and had finally settled on curling up with his head resting on her forearm.

She had finished her meal and had sat down when he made himself at home. The dogs didn't mind, they were used to cats. She and Maddie had had two cats, but both had died before Maddie. She thought about getting a cat but didn't want to deal with a litter box in the RV. The big cat was a good substitute. She liked the tranquility a cat brought when it sat on her lap and purred.

Austin heard the melodic sound of "yoo-hoo" and felt her heart skip a beat. She knew before the woman stepped into the light that it was the bookshop owner. Her voice sounded exactly as she expected, a melodic tone that spoke to her soul.

"I brought you some cookies to welcome you to the park. I hope you like chocolate-chip. I figured most people do so I took a shot," Jaime said as she looked around the campsite.

Austin could tell she was nervous because the little shopkeeper's eyes kept looking around the site and then at the cat in her lap and then back at the site. "I love chocolate-chip cookies. My name is Austin Stevens, by the way. If you're going to bring me cookies the least, I can do is tell you my name." Austin chuckled as the woman finally looked directly at her.

Jaime felt the vibrations of the woman's low dulcet tones from the bottom of her feet to the top of her head. She shivered and relished the tingling throughout her body that the timbre of the woman's voice elicited. The Amazon's voice was exactly as she imagined it and struck a chord deep in her soul.

As for Austin, she couldn't pull her eyes away, it was as if she were looking into a verdant landscape that immediately set her mind at ease and gave her the feeling of peace and of being loved. She kept staring until the woman said, "My cat seems to have found a home on your lap. I'm Jaime Crocket, by the way."

"Yes, he walked right in, snubbed my dogs and jumped up on my lap." She laughed as she continued to pet the cat.

Jaime's heart picked up a beat or two. The woman's laugh was deep and filled the bookshop owner's heart with a lightness and sense of safety she had never felt before. "Yes, well, he is a bit of a snob. He tolerates dogs and most people, but I must admit, it is a surprise that he's sitting on your lap." She looked at Titus with a raised eyebrow and he returned her stare as if daring her to make him move. "Your dogs are so well-behaved. Is it okay if I pet them?" she said as she gestured toward the pen.

"Go right ahead, they don't bite."

Jaime made her way over to the dogs and reached into the pen to pet their heads. They both looked up at her with adoration and leaned into her hands. The dogs seemed to be part chihuahua and something else. The female looked as if she descended from the miniature pinscher family of dogs. She was black with white socks and an overbite with a snaggle tooth. Jaime lost her heart to the dog right away. The male was golden brown and looked and acted like a Jack Russell terrier. He was jumping at her, trying to get her attention.

"Good dogs, you guys are so sweet. I bet you don't give your Mama any trouble, do you?" Jaime kept talking to the dogs and Austin watched her while stroking the cat. *Well, the dogs like her. That's a good sign*, Austin thought.

"Would you like to sit down? I could get us a glass of milk to go with the cookies." Austin gestured toward the other camp chair and stood, upsetting the cat and sending him leaping to the ground. She came back with two glasses of milk and sat them down on the small table between the two chairs.

"Oh no, I don't have to stay if I'm interrupting your evening. I wanted to welcome you to the park." Jaime stood up from leaning over the pen, which she thought sounded lame since she had already said as much. "I saw you pull in the other day and have been meaning to get over here, but you know how it is. Not enough time in the day."

"Well, you can't expect me to eat them by myself. If you do, I'll eat them all and be as big as this RV, you wouldn't want that on your conscience, would you? Besides I already got milk for us to drink with the cookies."

Jaime chuckled, "No, you're right I wouldn't want to have to worry about that at all."

They ate their cookies and drank their milk in silence, listening to the sound of crickets chirping and the fire crackling. Austin looked up at the stars and marveled how bright the stars made the night. One of the reasons she loved traveling in her RV was this kind of moment where the stars weren't encumbered by the ambient light of the city.

She noticed Jaime was doing the same thing. She felt as if she should say something, but she was enjoying the silence too much. It was nice to sit with someone and not have to talk, at least for a little while.

"So how did you end up at the Purple Cactus? Have you been RV-ing long?" The younger woman must have read her mind, but not saying anything wasn't going to happen, at least not tonight.

"About two years or so. I decided I was tired of moving around and wanted to settle in for a while." Austin knew she wasn't totally answering Jaime's question, but she didn't want to talk about how tired she was of being alone.

"What about you, how did you end up here at the Purple Cactus? What gave you the idea to open a bookshop? By the way, I think it's a great idea. I like to read and there have been a few nights when I was on the road that I wished I had a good book to read. Connecting to the internet is iffy at best in most of these places so if I couldn't download a book to my Kindle, I was out of luck."

"Well, let's see. I'm an avid reader as well and I love books. I appreciate the Kindle, but I like the feel and smell of a book, especially a new one. There's something to be said for hearing the crackle of fresh pages opening for the first time and the heft of the book in your hands. It feels as if I'm about to embark on a great adventure and I can't wait to get started. I hoped other people felt the same way, so I opened The Reading Nook." Jaime blushed as she realized she was being a nerd about books.

"Wow, I don't think I've heard reading a book described that way. You make me want to go out and buy a book right away."

Jaime huffed, "Uh-huh."

"No, it's true! I had never thought of reading that way. I guess I'm a novice when it comes to reading and books. I'm not a connoisseur like you. I download and I read. I don't think about the actual action of reading. You've given me something to think about. Thank you!"

Jaime wasn't sure if Austin was teasing her or not, but the way she was looking at her indicated she was serious.

After a moment, Jaime blinked and said, "In answer to the other question about ending up her at the Purple Cactus, I retired early from my job and wanted to travel. I didn't have anything or anyone keeping me home and you only live once so I sold everything, packed up, and bought myself a teardrop trailer that I pulled with my Jeep. I traveled around for a few years before I realized there might be a market for the bookshop and as they say, the rest is history. I had stayed here a few times and liked the park as well as the location, so I struck a deal with Rudy Wellman and here I am."

"Smart move from what I can tell. I've been traveling for a couple of years all over the United States and I love seeing new places. Getting to see parts of America, I wouldn't otherwise see has been fun and I realized early on in my travels this was the life for me. I wasn't ready to go back home to Texas, so I took this job when it opened up."

Jaime shifted in her seat to get a little closer to the Amazon. "It's seems to be a lot of labor-intensive work. How do you do it? I'm not sure I could do some of the things I've seen you do over the last week." Jaime blushed again. *What is wrong with me? We are having a simple conversation. Why do I keep blushing like a teenager?*

"I'm used to it. Before I started traveling, I worked in my family's landscaping business. I missed working too, so for me this is a win-win. I get to do some landscaping and if I get tired of living in one place, I can move on to another park." *What is going on with me? I don't think I've talked this much in five years with anyone new. Why is she so easy to talk to?* Austin thought as she looked into Jaime's eyes. *I want to drown in those eyes.*

"I for one am glad you're here," Jaime said.

Austin looked at her with a raised eyebrow.

"I mean to handle the landscaping. I worry Titus might run into one of our reptilian friends or other predators when he's out and about. He especially loves the tall grass so if you're keeping it down, I can sleep better at night." *Oh my god, I am so lame. Get it together, Jaime.*

Jaime glanced at her watch and saw it was already 10 p.m. She stood and said, "I better get going. I'm opening early in the morning. Why don't you come by for a cup of coffee?"

Austin turned and looked at her for the longest moment. Those green eyes were mesmerizing, and she was caught up in their intensity. "Ah, well, I'll see. I've got a lot to do in the morning, you know. I've got a long list of work to do and the list keeps gets longer and longer the more the time I spend here. And I do have a duty to keep Titus safe." Austin winked at the shopkeeper.

"Oh yes, of course," Jaime laughed; however, she was disappointed. She thought they had made a connection, but Austin seemed to be backing away. It had been a long time since she had sat in someone's company and made easy conversation. She spent all day talking to people, but with Austin their talking had felt like a real conversation, not superficial.

She picked up Titus from a spot by the fire. "Come on Titus, time to go home. Bye, Clara Jane and Rocky Bob, I'll be seeing you." She looked at Austin. "You're going to have to tell me how you came up with their names one of these days." The dogs stood up and wagged their tails, as if to say "See ya later."

"Bye, Austin." Austin stood and marveled at the small woman's ability to carry the cat without looking as if she were straining. She waved at Jaime as she walked away.

~~~~~

Austin worked at putting the fire out and tidying up the campsite before she turned in for the night. *Oh man – how stupid am I? I almost gave into having coffee with Jaime. Spending time with her would have been a bad idea. I am not in the market for another partner. Wait, what? Another partner? What am I thinking? No way! I've had my one true love and I know you only get one in a lifetime.*

"Right dogs? Dogs?" Austin turned toward her dogs. They were both lying down with their heads on their beds. If they could talk, they'd say "You keep denying your feelings and maybe one day someone will believe you." She absently grabbed the necklace around her neck carrying her wedding ring.

She had vowed to Maddie she would never take the ring off. After Maddie died, wearing the symbol of their devotion on her finger was too much. She had compromised and hung the ring on a necklace. She never took the icon off and over the last five years the necklace had provided comfort to her when she was feeling lonely and missing her partner.

"I know, I know, she was cute, and her cookies were to die for, but what about Maddie? I know you guys didn't know her, but believe me, this is not a good idea," she said to the dogs as she reached down and opened the latch of the dog pen.

"Come on, you guys let's go to bed." Austin threw some dirt on the fire, gathered her two dogs, and took them inside. A few minutes later the light went off in the living room of her RV.

The wind was blowing, and Austin lay in her bed, feeling the RV rock. The first few nights in a new place always made her jittery. She wasn't sure why, but she did love the wind, the whistling and rocking reminded her of home. Thoughts of home always seemed to bring her comfort.

She heard the crack of a branch and knew she would find kindling for her fire in the morning. As she listened to the wind, the rocking motion of the RV settled her nerves. Jaime was an interesting woman, the first woman she had had any interest in since Maddie. "Since Maddie!" Austin said as she felt tears stream down her face. She was so lonely and missed her so much.

"How did my life end up this way?" she moaned to herself. "I can't believe I'm in Arizona, away from everything I know, my family, my friends -- well not many friends, I guess I let most of them fall by the wayside after Maddie died." Thinking about her family made her homesick. She missed her Dad and her brothers. She was tempted to pack up and leave the next day but running back home wouldn't do any good. She'd still feel the same way. She wanted to change her life and it was the main reason she had left. She wanted to feel differently. The wind continued into the night and at some point, rain began to fall. The gentle patter of rain on her roof lulled Austin to sleep.

STOPPING THE CRACKS

"Oh, man -- how stupid am I? I can't believe I invited Austin to coffee in the morning. I don't know anything about her Titus, except I haven't been comfortable with someone in a long time." Jaime mumbled as she hefted the cat up a little more on her hip as she made her way back to her trailer.

The night was pitch-black and juggling her flashlight and the cat was making walking difficult. And the light did not seem to be penetrating the inky darkness. She could hear the swish of wings in the air as she walked along. The bats were out hunting mosquitoes.

This was one of her favorite times, the moments between the ending of a day and the beginning of a new day. She did her best thinking at this time. As a child and into her young adult life, this was the time when she could be alone with her thoughts. As she grew older, she relished this time. Even when she had someone in her life, she would separate herself and take a few moments for contemplation or reflection.

One thing I know, I have got to get to know her better. She has tried to hide her sadness, but her sorrow is written all over her face. I wonder what happened to her and why she was so sad? Jaime thought as she arrived at her RV and opened the door. Titus jumped into the RV and moved off to his bed on the top bunk over the driver's seat.

"Okay, go to bed. I don't care, ya mangy cat. I was trying to have a conversation with you, but oh no, you have more important things to do . . . like sleep," Jaime harrumphed.

She continued to think about her evening with Austin and how comfortable she felt with the Amazon. They seemed to fit. Their conversation had been easy. Surprisingly, she was comforted by Austin. She had never felt this way around other people, even Oscar. Adulthood had been the turning point for her relationship with Oscar. Now, she was totally comfortable sharing her hopes and dreams with him. She had spent only a few hours with Austin, and she was dumbfounded at the way she felt. She knew in her heart that sharing her inner thoughts would be like coming home.

As she was performing her nightly ritual of a hot shower, she took apart her feelings for Austin

Stevens. The woman was attractive, with those piercing blue eyes and the way they reflected her pain. She tried to hide the fractures, but Jaime could see them. They reminded her of the miniscule cracks caused by pebbles hitting a windshield.

At first, they are small and don't appear to be a problem, but a change in atmosphere causes the cracks to extend across the whole windshield. She wanted to be the one to keep the cracks from getting bigger. She knew in the depths of her soul that she was the one who could help Austin. The questions she asked were, how was she supposed to help her, and would the Amazon let her?

The water began to cool as Jaime put her thoughts aside for the moment. One of the things she'd done when she bought the RV was to make the shower bigger, which meant giving up storage space. She loved bathing at night. Getting clean and then crawling into bed was a luxury for her. When she was younger, getting clean was not always possible. Her life in the foster-care system had not been easy. She was always having to fight for shower time and most of the time she lost. She had made herself a promise that as soon as she was old enough and could afford her own way, she would never go without getting clean before she went to bed.

As she crawled into her bed, a vision of Austin appeared in her mind. Sitting in her chair and petting Titus. She was handsome, Jane was right. Handsome was the best word to describe the Amazon's looks. She was intrigued and wanted, no needed, to know more about her. *Why was this woman sad? What was her favorite color? Did she have any children? Was she married? Was she a lesbian? How was she going to find out about her?* Questions whirled around in her head until she finally drifted off to sleep, dreaming of a blue-eyed Amazonian woman.

Jaime woke to a beautiful morning. She could hear the birds singing and Titus had managed to snuggle his way into her armpit. She reached over and kissed his head, stroking his back as she lay in bed thinking about Austin. It had been a long time since she was intrigued by a woman. Her thoughts danced in her head as she took stock of the woman and her feelings.

She was attracted to "the handsome Amazon" the pet name she had come up with the night before. As she watched her over the previous week, she had been drawn to her more and more. The night before had been a culmination of her wanting to meet Austin and her natural curiosity to find out something about her. Jaime realized she had not found out anything of importance about Austin except she was comfortable with her and was absolutely attracted to her.

"I guess we better get up and get going, the bookshop is not going to open by itself, besides I'm ready for some coffee. Let's go, Titus, move over, I'll give you some food." She pushed on the cat to get him to move off the bed. He resisted for a minute and then allowed her to push him off the bed. He wanted her to know he was moving because he wanted to, not because she wanted him to move.

Jaime got up and made her way into the kitchen area. She checked Titus' water fountain, making sure he had plenty of water and pulled open a drawer under the refrigerator where the cat's bowls were housed. She put kibbles into both of his bowls. He walked over and proceeded to chow down, which was a good descriptor for how he ate. Most cats were dainty eaters, but Titus was part Maine Coon and he was almost as big as a dog, which required him to eat a lot more food than a normal cat. Jaime fed him twice a day and it seemed as if he continued to grow.

"Wow! Titus, you keep growing and I'm going to have to put you outside permanently." The cat looked at her, daring her to relegate him to the outside.

"I'm teasing, big guy. How'd I get so lucky to have a cat-dog as my pet." The cat turned and looked at her with a smirk. He knew he was king of the park and felt as if she should treat him that way.

Jaime busied herself with getting ready for the day. She picked out a pair of cut-offs, no doubt inspired by Austin, and a T-shirt saying "I Like Naps" with a sloth on the front. The shirt was one of her favorites and she wore it as often as she could. Her Birkenstocks came next and she was ready to go.

As she opened the front door, she breathed in the fresh air. "What a lovely morning, Titus! I think today's going to be perfect. And we got rain last night! I bet the flowers and trees are so happy." She stepped down and reveled in the beauty surrounding her. She marveled at the blueness of the sky, she could hear the birds singing in the new day and the stream was no longer tinkling, but bubbling. She nodded her head accepting the new day and made her way over to her bookshop.

Jaime unlocked the padlock and pressed the button to raise the door and open the book shop to the public. Once the door was out of the way, she rolled out a rug and began setting furniture around the area. She watched as Austin approached from the road. The dogs were following behind her and she seemed to be deep in thought. "Hi, Austin, hope you had a good night's rest." Austin looked up as if startled from a daydream and gave her a wave. No smile, no move to come talk to her. She kept on walking.

Damn, I wish I knew what was going on with that woman. Jaime watched her walk out of sight and turned to the "Hello" of one of her early morning customers.

~~~~~

Austin struggled with her feelings as she walked along. She was tired of feeling sad and alone but couldn't seem to get past her feelings. Her life kept moving along, but she felt as if she were drifting. Jaime was the first person in a long time who held her interest. She wanted to get to know her, she really did, but she couldn't get past the guilt of betraying Maddie -- and the dreams she kept having didn't help.

Every time she seemed to make strides toward moving on, she would dream about Maddie again. She heard Jaime wish her a good morning but couldn't bring herself to say anything. *She was a fraud. She didn't have any business stringing this woman along. Wait, stringing her along? What was she thinking? She didn't even know the woman,* Austin thought as she strolled down the path, but if she was honest with herself, a long time had passed since she had sat with someone and felt totally comfortable.

She had to admit she was perplexed by the comfort she felt in the bookshop owner's company. She had tried to hide her pain but felt as if she failed. She had caught Jaime looking at her a couple of times with a look of contemplation. She thought the petite woman would say something during their conversation, but she didn't. Austin had been relieved. She didn't want to talk about Maddie or her pain or anything relating to her past love. She wanted to bask in the comfort coming from Jaime. Her soul has been soothed for a short time last night. She had almost forgotten about her pain and grief. Almost.

The path turned and she found herself down by the stream. The atmosphere was so peaceful, exactly what she needed. The water flowed over the rocks, creating a bubbling sound. As she looked farther down the stream, she could see a small pool had formed. As she moved along the stream bed, she could see small fish darting among the rocks.

The dogs ran along side of her, jumping in and out of the water, chasing the fish and digging their paws in the crevices where the fish were trying to hide. As she neared the pool, she could see it was a few feet deep, perfect for whiling away a hot summer day. She made a mental note to come back to this spot on one of her days off. Hopefully, this hidden treasure wouldn't evaporate as the days heated up.

Cottonwood trees provided shade on both sides of the stream. The web had long been abandoned and nearly torn to shreds by the wind and last night's rain. There was enough space for her to walk along the edge of the stream, but the grass was thick and she knew she would need to mow it to keep the people visiting the park safe from unwanted reptiles and other critters. The grass was a refuge from the sun, cool and moist.

A natural bridge of stones in the water made crossing to the other side easy. She could hear birds singing in the trees and the fresh scent of rain permeated the air. Even though the grass was thick, the section she stumbled upon had an area cleared naturally and would be a wonderful place for her and the dogs to play.

To test her theory, she picked up a stick and threw it toward the water. Both dogs leaped into the stream, trying to beat the other one to the makeshift toy. She laughed at their antics. One of them would bring the stick back and then the other would fetch and return it. The dogs seemed to be enjoying taking turns bringing the stick back to their mistress. Both wanted her praise for getting the stick. Each time they came back, they would shake off and cover her with water. The shower was refreshing even if she did eventually smell like a wet dog.

"Come on you guys, let's head back. I'm going to have to give you a bath to get rid of the smell. I'm glad they have a dog wash. You guys are going to love all the attention I'm going to shower on you. Get it, shower?" She laughed to herself as she climbed up the embankment. Both dogs stopped moving and growled. She almost stepped on them. She had begun her climb walking through the grass.

"What's up Clara, Rocky?" She was about to take another step, when she heard a rattle coming from the grasses in the direction she was stepping. She slowly lowered her leg and took a step back. With the throwing stick, she moved the grass and nestled in the undergrowth was a rattler's nest. Unfortunately, she confirmed what she suspected. The grass was a great place for the unwanted reptiles to hang out. A perfect place to hide from predators hunting them.

"Oh, my gosh, thank goodness you guys warned me. I wouldn't have liked getting bit by a snake. Come on, let's give her a wide berth." She and the dogs backtracked down the embankment and walked over to the natural path heading back to the main part of the camp.

As she made her way back into the RV camp, she saw Jaime waiting on a good-looking man. She seemed to be enthralled with every word he was saying. *Did I get it wrong? Does she play for the other team? Why is he getting all her attention?* She debated about going over to talk to Jaime but decided to return to her campsite. Besides, she had work to do and needed to check in with Jane and get the projects she needed to take care of for the day.

~~~~~

Oscar was going on about his latest date, when Jaime noticed Austin walking by. She was drenched and the dogs looked the same. *They must have found the stream. I hope she didn't run into any rattlers. I should have warned her about the snakes last night,* Jaime thought as she tuned Oscar out.

She continued to watch Austin walk down the road until she was out of sight. It seemed to Jane as if she were spending a lot of time watching Austin walk around the park. *Well, she is a nice, cool drink of water as Oscar so eloquently put it the other day. I wonder, why she's avoiding me? What is going on in that handsome head of yours, my Amazon? Hold up, she* *is not <u>your</u> Amazon, at least not yet. Yes, you know you want her to be. Oh yes, yes, I do.*

"James, are you paying attention to me? I'm regaling you about my splendid date last night and you don't seem to be interested at all. I'm hurt," Oscar said with a pretend frown on his face.

"I'm sorry, Oscar. I can't figure this new woman out. I took her some cookies last night, you know, to welcome her to the park."

"Of course, you did."

"Hey, I thought it was the least I could do. She doesn't know anybody, and I was trying to be friendly." She frowned at him.

"Of course, you were."

"Would you stop interrupting me? I'm trying to talk to you." She stomped her foot and he grinned at her antics.

"I'm sorry," Oscar said as he took a sip of his coffee. "So, tell me everything, what was she like, did you find out anything about her?"

"Well, that's the thing. We talked, which was great, but I didn't really get to know her. I know she's been RVing for a while and she had a landscape business with her family, but that's about it. And here's the crazy thing, when I got to her camp Titus was sitting in her lap. Have you known Titus to sit in anyone's lap?" Oscar raised an eyebrow.

"Really, that cat doesn't like anyone and by anyone, I mean me. I don't know how many times I've tried to pet him, and he swipes at me. It's a wonder I don't have tons of scars from all the scratches he's directed my way." He looked at his hands looking for imaginary scars.

"Don't be such a baby, he loves you in his own way," Jaime said as she squeezed his shoulder.

"Right, you keep telling yourself that. So, nothing, no good gossip about her?"

"Oscar, I don't gossip. The only other thing I learned was that her name is Austin and she has two dogs, Clara Jane and Rocky Bob." She grinned as she told him the names.

"Oh my god, are those really her dogs' names?" he asked incredulously.

Jaime started laughing, "Yes, I think it's a Texas thing. To give your pets more than one name. They are so cute and well behaved. They didn't even bark at me when I walked into her camp."

"Well, honey, it sounds as if we need to do a little investigating. Don't you have dinner tonight with Barney?" He rubbed his hands together, hatching a plan for Jaime to get the information she needed about Austin.

"Yes, I do, but I don't know, it doesn't seem right to quiz Barney." She screwed her face up, contemplating whether it was a good idea to question her surrogate father.

"Of course, it's right. You need to know who the new gal is in the park. I mean, you are practically the mayor of the park. It's your duty."

"No, I'm not," Jaime said, shaking her head.

"Yes, you are. Everyone looks to you for help and advice, plus you are the only person who has a business in here beside Pete -- and making breakfast on the weekend doesn't count." Jaime thought about what Oscar was saying and he wasn't totally off the mark. She should find out what she could about Austin, and she knew Barney would keep her confidence.

"Okay, I'll see what I can find out, but don't get your hopes up. Barney may not know anything, either." She picked up Oscar's empty cup, refilled it one more time and poured herself one. She was going to need a boost to question the old man.

DADDY'S GIRL

Austin was finishing the dinner dishes when her phone rang. "Hey there, baby girl, how's my SugarPop doin'?"

"Hiya, Daddy, I'm good."

"Are you gettin' settled in okay? Ready for your ole man to come visit?" Buckston knew driving to Arizona was going to be a long trip, but he missed his daughter and with his son Junior sharing the drive it wouldn't be too bad, or at least he hoped it wouldn't be too bad. His hips bothered him when he traveled long distances in a truck, but he didn't like to fly, and his son's vehicle was comfortable enough.

"Sure am, whenever you want, you know you're welcome." Austin felt a hint of excitement, as she missed her father as much as he missed her.

"Well, I was thinkin' I might get your brother Junior to drive me over at the end of the week, and maybe stay for a week. Would that work for you?"

The uncertainty could be heard in his voice over the phone.

"Sure, come on over. You know, I've got plenty of room for you and Junior. Are you up for the drive? It's a long way and with your hips, I don't want you to be in a lot of pain while you're here." Austin worried about her Dad, he wasn't getting any younger, but she knew when he made his mind up there was no stopping him. *Kind of like me.*

After a brief pause, she said, "Are you guys goin' to want to do some fishin'? We've got a stream close to the park, but I don't think there's catchable fish in it. The dogs and I were out at the stream here by the park today, but it's not deep enough for real fish."

"I was thinkin' about it, think you can find us a spot?" She could see her Dad rubbing his hands together in anticipation of the age-old struggle of man vs. fish.

"I'll see what I can do. I met this guy named Barney Wilton who runs a horseback-riding ranch. I bet he knows of a place we can go fishin'. I'll give him a call and see what I can find out for us."

"That's my girl." There was a hesitation and Austin thought, *oh no, here it comes.*

"Listen, baby girl, are you still havin' those dreams?" She could hear the concern in his voice, it was sweet, but irritating as well.

"Daddy, I told you, I'm okay. You don't need to concern yourself with my dreams," She said in a huff.

"Sugar, I love you and my heart breaks to see ya so sad all the time. What can I do? It's been five years since we lost Maddie. I know getting over heartbreak takes a while to get back into the swing of things, but you're still a young woman. You should be living your life not waiting for life to happen." Buckston had been trying since Maddie died to get Austin to share with him the dreams that were holding her hostage from living her life, but she was stubborn like him and didn't want to burden him.

"Daddy, there's nothing you can do. It's just going to take time. Maybe five years isn't long enough. Look at you, you never remarried." There was a pause and Austin could see in her mind's eye her Dad trying to come up with a comment, but she knew he couldn't because she was right. She also knew he was trying to make her feel better.

"Okay, honey. I'm here for you if you need to talk. I'm lookin' forward to seein' ya." He knew the best offense was to retreat.

"Me too, Daddy. Tell Junior to come by himself. I don't want him to bring his latest conquest. I want it to be us. I'd like to spend time with both of you without any kind of competition for Junior's attention." She heard her father guffaw.

"Okay, baby doll, you got it. Talk to you soon, I love you."

"I love you too, Daddy. Bye." Austin put down her phone and thought about her Father. He had raised her and her brothers all alone from the time she was seven. Her mother had died in a car accident and her Dad, Buckston Lee Stevens, had been devastated, but knew he had to carry on.

It was tough in the beginning. He was raised with the idea that the man took care of the family with his job and the wife took care of the family. When his wife died, so did that idea. He had one little girl and two boys to take care of. They needed his undivided attention so he hunkered down and did the best he could. He hired a housekeeper to take care of the house because he still needed to work, but he ended his day at 5 p.m. so he could be home at night with the kids.

He had dated a few women while the kids were growing up, but as soon as they tried to settle in, he'd give them the boot. Right after Maddie died Austin had asked him why he never remarried. He answered, "Honey, I believe there is only one person in the world for me and that was your Mama. No one else will ever measure up so I decided to stay single."

Austin took that to heart, and she had been following the same path as her Father. But somehow that didn't seem to fit for her, especially after meeting Jaime. She loved Maddie with her whole heart and to think about giving it to someone else didn't seem to make sense. She needed to focus on her job and not worry about what was going on with Jaime. Her Dad was right. There was only one woman for her -- and that was Maddie.

~~~~~

Jaime drove over to Barney's on her scooter. She had a Jeep, but the scooter has a softer footprint and being budget conscious, she tried to save money. Riding her scooter cost her next to nothing in gas. Besides, the high desert was beautiful most nights so riding the scooter was the way to go as far as she was concerned. She loved her scooter; the miniature motorcycle was her baby, bright white with black accents. The scooter was a 125 so she could drive anywhere including around the park and even into town. Her carryall on the back had enough room for the casserole she had made for the rancher, along with a salad.

Barney usually had beer, which was fine with her. She enjoyed a beer every now and then, not as much as she liked wine or Irish whiskey, but it would do in a pinch. She pulled into the drive by his small, ranch-style house and parked by the porch. The porch covered the whole expanse of the front of the house and she loved it.

The old man had put a porch swing on one side and comfortable chairs with a table on the other side, perfect for after-dinner whiskey. No flowers or kitschy decorations, but Jaime felt the lack of decoration suited Barney and his personality. He was a no-nonsense guy and she appreciated him. She was counting on his directness to find out as much as she could about Austin. Jaime felt a tiny bit guilty, but figured this was her best shot to get some information about the Amazon, especially since Austin was not making herself available to have this discussion.

The rest of his place reflected who he was at heart. The ranch was simple, with a barn and a couple of horse paddocks. She took off her helmet and laid it on top of the seat. She heard the horses whinny and made her way over to the fenced area. He had two horses that stayed close to the barn, Sadie and Missy. They were the horses he used for the kids to ride as they were both gentle giants. Both horses put their heads over the fencing, instinctively knowing that Jaime would have a treat for them.

"Hello, Ladies, how are you this evening?" She gave each a couple of bites of carrots from her pockets and rubbed them both under the chin. They both loved chin rubs.

The rancher stepped out with his hound dog, Buster, to greet her. "Hey there, Jaime. How are you tonight? I'm starving! I see you gave the girls some attention." Jaime chuckled. Barney said that same thing to her every Tuesday night when she brought over dinner.

"See ya later, Ladies, your Daddy's calling me." The horses whinnied and turned around to make their way back over to the hay laid out for them to munch on.

"Hey Barney, I've got your favorite." She grinned as she made her way back to the scooter. She walked behind the scooter and opened the carryall to gather the food.

"Chicken casserole?" The hungry man said while rubbing his hands together.

"You got it. I brought a salad, too." She walked toward the porch and handed him the salad as she climbed the two steps to the landing.

"Great, I've got the table set and some beer in the fridge. I bought your favorite, Blue Moon. I'm going to stick to Coors, though. That stuff you drink tastes terrible." He grimaced as he opened the door to his house.

"Oh, Barney, you didn't need to do that, I like Coors too." She meant it, but if cornered, she had to admit she thought Coors was weak and tasted watered down.

"I know you do, but I wanted to get you something special because you're so nice to me," the horseman grumbled as he walked into the kitchen. Jaime chuckled and followed him. She had been coming to his house for so long she knew where he kept most everything. She grabbed a big spoon for the casserole and some salad tongs. He had scoffed when she bought him the tongs, but she knew he appreciated the gesture.

They sat down at the kitchen table that had a red and white checked tablecloth and mis-matched plates. In the center was a batch of wildflowers. "Barney, the table looks lovely, what's the special occasion?"

"Nothing really, just thought it might be a nice touch," Barney said bashfully. Jaime was touched by his efforts. The man was almost eighty and his interest in her was purely fatherly. "Well, you know I never had any kids and you're about as close as

I'm going to get. I thought it wouldn't kill me to make an effort for you."

Jaime smiled at him and patted him on the back. "You know how to make me feel special. Thank you for going to the trouble, it means a lot to me." At that moment, Buster made himself known with a loud howl. Jaime laughed, "You too, Buster. I love you, too." He wagged his tail and took his place by the stove.

They started to eat and for a few moments, the only noise was the clink of silverware. After a few minutes, Jaime took a drink of her beer and asked, "So Barney, what do you think about the new gal over at the park? I met her the other night and she seems like she's real nice." *Way to go James, obvious much?* she thought as she eyed him over her beer bottle, trying to gauge if he knew she was fishing for information.

"Oh yeah, she's really nice. She came highly recommended. You know my pal, Gus, over in Amarillo, well he told me about her. She worked up there in one of the parks for a few months and everybody liked her. You know she's a Texan." Jaime smiled to herself. If you were from anywhere in Texas, you were good no matter what, according to Barney. He thought people from Arizona were crazy because of the heat and people from Colorado were crazy because of the cold even though he had settled in Arizona, which had both. She didn't have the heart to tell him she was from Oklahoma; he might kick her out of his house if he knew she was born there and had moved to Arizona when she was five.

"Well, that's good to know. I was worried for a minute. Not being from Texas would worry me, too." Jaime teased him as she took a bite of her salad. "Hmm … she's worked in RV parks before? That's good. We need somebody stable to stay. I didn't think we would find someone on such short notice," she said with the right amount of curiosity in her voice.

"Yeah well, she was looking for a new place to be. She had been traveling around for the last few years and the Amarillo spot was temporary." Barney said as he took another bite of his casserole.

"Makes sense. Did Gus say anything about her people?" Jaime cringed, as she hated to use that type of phrase, but the man was old school, so he understood what she meant.

"Yeah, her Daddy worked in the oil business and was a rodeo man. I guess she's pretty close to him, being as she's the only girl." Barney continued to eat and drink in between his comments.

"Really, the only girl. How many brothers does she have?" She was getting a gold-mine of information from the old gossip. Men gossiping always surprised her sometimes. They were bigger gossips than women. For a second, she felt guilty, but she justified her questioning with the idea that she was trying to be a good neighbor. *Yeah, right, Crocket, this is not about being a good neighbor, this is about you being nosy and trying to find out as much as you can about your Amazon.*

"Well, Gus didn't know for sure, but he thought two." She looked at him in surprise.

"Wow, two brothers and her being the only girl. No wonder she's close to her Dad. What about her Mom?" She was intrigued and couldn't seem to stop the questions.

"Gus told me she died when Austin was a little girl. Such a shame, little girls need their Momma's," Barney said as he finished up his meal.

"Yes, I suppose they do." Jaime bent her head so the old man wouldn't see the longing in her eyes. Part of the reason she moved to Arizona was to come live with her Grandmother after her parents died, but her Grandmother had died suddenly a year later from a heart attack. Jaime had grown up in foster care and she didn't have a regular family.

"Oh, I'm sorry Honey. I didn't mean to bring up bad feelings." Her wannabe surrogate father leaned over to pat her on the shoulder, regretting what he had said. He knew about her upbringing, as she had shared with him her story not long after she started bringing him dinner. She was not one to dwell on the past and since they had become friends and her feelings for him had grown, she felt she should tell him about her life.

"It's okay Barney, I've got you and Oscar as my family and that's all I need." She reassured him as she pushed her plate away.

"That Oscar is nothing but trouble if you ask me," Barney said with a tiny smile. He loved Oscar too, he didn't like to admit it, but he did. "Anyway, she's close to her family, but it seems she lost someone about five years ago that devastated her. Gus wasn't sure who it was, but he said she was sad most of the time they worked together." He paused for a moment and then continued. "He really liked her. Said she was a hard worker and never shirked from anything he asked her to do." Jaime could hear the admiration in his voice. One thing Barney appreciated was a hard worker.

"Well, I'm glad she's here. We need someone like her," Jaime said as she stood to collect the dishes and take them to the sink. She helped Barney with the dishes and sat with him on the front porch for a while drinking whiskey and enjoying the sounds of the night. As it neared 9 p.m., she said her goodbyes. As she drove back to the park, she pondered what kind of loss could have made Austin so sad.

FAMILY MEANS EVERYTHING

The next two weeks went by fast for both women. Austin spent her time creating a daily routine and getting to know the people who were coming and going. And Jaime continued to watch her from afar as she served coffee and wine to her patrons. Oscar came by a few times to visit, which made the days go faster. Jaime was dying to get to know Austin better, but it seemed as if Austin was avoiding her. As soon as she would turn Austin's way, Austin would head in a separate direction. Titus was still going over to Austin's campsite, but Jaime had not got up enough nerve to go back to her site.

The end of the week arrived and with it came Austin's Dad, Buckston, and her brother, Buckston Jr. The big truck pulled into the park a little after noon on Friday. Both men got out of the truck and proceeded to stretch in the same way. Jaime was mesmerized by the display. They looked and acted the same. She could see the resemblance to Austin right away and knew they had to be her father and brother.

Both men had strong jawlines and dizzying height. However, Austin's jaw was a softer version of her Father and brother. As they walked around the truck, both their gaits matched Austin's down to the slight bow of their legs. They had crew cuts, whereas Austin cut her hair so short she almost looked bald. Jaime decided she liked the look the Stevens family portrayed.

Austin came running from the vicinity of the stream, with both dogs trailing behind. She threw herself into her Dad's arms and Jaime couldn't help but wish she was the one getting such an obviously happy hello. Austin turned to her brother and did the same thing. Both men hugged and kissed her on the cheek, holding her at arm's length to get a good look at her. Even from a distance, Jaime could see the genuine affection both men had for her Amazon.

Austin looked at her Dad and brother and was so happy to see them. She even forgot she was avoiding Jaime. "Hey, Jaime, come meet my Dad and brother!"

Jaime looked around her shop and since no one was there, she made her way over to Austin and her family. "Hello Sir, I'm Jaime Crocket, I run the bookshop over there. So nice to meet you." Jaime stuck out her hand to shake Buckston's hand.

"Nice to meet you, ma'am, this is my son Buckston Jr., or Junior for short." Jaime turned and shook his hand as well. Junior looked her up and down and grinned. The Steven's grin was one most women could not resist. Jaime smiled back and Austin groaned inwardly. Another conquest for her brother, her worst nightmare.

"Well, I guess you probably need to get back to work, come on Dad, Junior, I'll show you around."

Jaime gave Austin a startled look. Pull, then push. She was never going to understand this woman. "Yes, you're right. I need to get back to it. Nice to meet ya'll. Hopefully, I'll see you soon. Come on over for a glass of wine later, if you feel like it."

"We sure will," replied Junior.

Austin watched Jaime walk away and fortunately, her eyes were hidden by the brim of her hat or Junior would have seen the death ray she shot his way. As he, too, watched Jaime walk away. Both siblings admiring the backside of the book shop owner.

"Junior, put your eyes back in your head," Buckston commented as he slapped his son on the back of his head.

"Well, Buttercup, let's see your new spread." He gestured as he looked around the park.

"Dad, it's not a spread, it's a park and I'm just working here. It's not mine," Austin said as she watched Jaime walk back toward her bookshop, feeling a bit embarrassed at the way she dismissed the little bookshop owner, but loving the way her butt swayed as she walked.

"I know darlin', but you'll make this place your own in no time." He winked at her and slapped Junior on the back, urging him forward.

"Yeah, Sis, give us a tour of the place you're calling home."

"Follow me, it's a nice-sized park, but the best part is my spot and the stream behind it. It's so peaceful. Daddy, I know you're going to love it." Austin led the way back to her campsite with both men trailing behind.

"I've got one of the biggest sites, since I'm living here full time. Don't you love the trees? My rig is always shaded, and I've managed to make the place feel like home," Austin said as they neared her place.

"Oh wow, Sis, this place is great. I'm glad I came with Dad, I was afraid there wouldn't be enough room for me, but I can see I was wrong."

"Austin, you done good. I couldn't have pictured a better place for you if I had tried, which by the way I did," Buckston said with laugh. He looked around the campsite. Austin had set up her outdoor kitchen to the right of her door making it easy access to bring items from the inside kitchen. She had a fire ring with four chairs and there was firewood stacked up under the RV to protect it from the elements.

"Hey, Sis, did you split the wood yourself?"

"No, the park provides it for free, since I work here. We have a barn at the back of the park, where we keep all the park equipment and a big stack of firewood. Customers can pay five bucks for ten pieces of wood. It's a good setup and a deal for the customers." Austin said with pride.

Buckston looked at his daughter and could see some of the pain lines had evaporated with her move to this park. *Boy, howdy, I'm glad she's doing well. I didn't know what I was going to do if this didn't work out for her.*

"Good, I'm looking forward to sitting by the fire this evening."

"You got it Dad, what do you think about my place?" She looked at her Dad like she did when she was a little girl. Not unlike most little girls, she was always looking for her Daddy's approval.

"Well, Sugar, I love it. You've laid it out well and if I was younger I would be putting myself in the hammock over there for a long afternoon nap, but if I did, you and your brother would have to get a backhoe to get me back out." They all laughed at the image of Buckston trying to get out of the hammock.

Secretly, Austin was pleased. She had thought the hammock was a great idea. Most of the staff at the park had caught her napping with the dogs at one time or another especially during the late afternoon.

"Well, I love your little napping nest and I'm glad I only have to fight one of you for napping rights."

The Stevens family was notorious for taking naps. When asked about their afternoon siestas, they all said the same thing, "Everyone should take a nap, resting gives you an extra umph to make it through the rest of the day." The practice was something their Mother instilled in them at a very young age and Buckston carried on the tradition.

"Let me tell ya, you're going to be hard pressed to beat me to a nap, Sis. In fact, I think I'll take a nap right now. Travelin' all day was tiring and wore me out. I could use the rest before dinner," Junior said as he sat down, kicking his boots off as he shifted around to get comfortable.

Austin stepped over and picked up his abandoned boots and put them on the seat of the picnic table. "Be careful brother, we have all kinds of critters that wouldn't mind making a home in your smelly boots." She wrinkled her nose for effect.

"Ha. You're so funny." He gave himself a push and let the swinging of the hammock lull him to sleep.

"Come on, Daddy, you must be tired too. I've got the bed in the back ready for you to take a nap." Buckston followed her into the RV.

"Now, Honeybun, I don't want to push you out of your bed."

"No problem, Daddy. I've got my recliner here and this chair is as comfortable as my bed. I'll be sleeping there, and I'll make up the overhead for Junior unless he wants to sleep outside."

"Well, you never know about your brother. He might decide to sleep in the back of his truck. He's got enough stuff in there to make it comfortable." She laughed along with her Father. It was a long-standing joke that Junior was always prepared and could make himself a bed anywhere.

~~~~~

Irritated, Jaime walked away from meeting Austin's Dad and brother. How was she going to break through to Austin, if she wouldn't give her the time of day? She had to figure out a way to get Austin to loosen up. *Maybe I could befriend her Dad. No, nope -- wouldn't be right.* She needed to talk to someone about this.

When she got back to her shop, the place was still deserted, which was not unusual for early afternoon. People were out hiking or boating or any of the other outdoor things available to do. She picked up her phone and dialed the number to her friend Sarah Gardner. She had befriended her when she set up shop in the park. Sarah had been the park attendant before Austin.

Sarah had come over immediately and introduced herself and her little dog Lola, when Jaime first arrived at the Purple Cactus. Lola and Titus had not gotten along. Lola was always yapping at the big cat. The cat tolerated the dog until he had had enough and then it had only taken one swipe with his paw on her backside and she had stayed away from him. Jaime still laughed about it when she thought of the little dog and the noise it made when Titus got hold of her. The entire park heard the wails, but granted, the dog was overreacting as there was no wound at all on her backside.

Sarah had been at the park for six months and knew all the ins and outs needed for Jaime to make her business a success. She had introduced her to Barney, who in turn had helped her negotiate with Rudy for the spot where she parked her shop. Rudy had wanted to put her off to the side out of the way of traffic, but Barney called him on his antics. Jaime had been grateful and that is what had started her Tuesday evening dinners with the old horse rancher.

The phone rang a couple of times. "Helloooo," The woman answered with a sing-songy inflection in her salutation. Jaime could hear a dog barking in the background and shook her head. Sarah's dog was always barking at something, even when the woman was working at the RV park. It was annoying, especially when she wanted to sleep in. The dog would start barking as soon as Sarah got up and let her out unless Titus was around and then she didn't hear a peep out of the dog. She started letting Titus out early so she could sleep in.

"Hiya, Sarah, it's Jaime," she said as she sat down at one of her tables.

"Shush, Lola!" She yelled and spoke at the same time. "Jaime, I'm so excited you called. It's been awhile. Lola, hush, now!" She could imagine Sarah wagging her finger at the dog and the dog ignoring her, like the little rascal did when she was at the park.

"I know, I'm a bad friend. I've been meaning to call you, but one thing leads to another and then it's time for bed and too late to call. How are you doing?" She said sipping her wine.

"You are not a bad friend and I'm doing fine. I miss the park, but coming home was the best thing I could do for my Momma. She's struggling with forgetting things and it's getting worse every day. I'm trying to help her the best I can, but I've had to hire someone come to help three days a week." There was a pause. "Never mind about me, how are you? Any new women come to the park you're interested in?" Jaime could picture the grin on her friend's face. Sarah and Oscar were always putting their heads together to find Jaime the perfect woman -- much to Jaime's chagrin.

"As a matter of fact, the woman who took your place. She is so handsome," Jaime said without thinking about what she was saying. She heard Sarah laugh on the other end of the line.

"Oscar and I worked so hard and all it took was for me to leave. So fine, hmm ... like a nice frosty cold beer or smooth red wine." Jaime paused for a minute and thought about Austin and her interactions with her so far. *Yep, still the same, whiskey all the way.*

"Actually, she's more like a fine Irish whiskey. A little bit of a bite, but smooth going down."

Sarah laughed, "Well, this sounds interesting. Why a bite?"

Jaime grimaced at the phone, "Well, the first week she was here I took her some cookies, and we seemed to hit it off right away."

"Of course, you did."

Jaime looked at the phone with a sense of Deja vu. "Hey, what does that mean? Oscar said the same thing."

"I mean you want people to feel welcome, so you always do something to welcome them. Although, baking cookies is a first. If you remember, you brought me a nice bottle of white wine."

"Well, of course, I want people to feel good. And cookies seemed like a good call. She felt like a cookie person to me just like you felt like a white-wine person."

"Okay, we'll get back to your premonitions about what people would or wouldn't like. Tell me about this woman."

Jaime smiled to herself and said, "OMG, Sarah, she is my dream woman, she's an Amazon. Or at least, the dream woman I didn't know I wanted until I met her. She's in her early fifties, but you can't tell unless you look at her hair, which is gray, but she keeps it short. Short -- almost bald -- but on her the hairdo looks good. She has a perfect shaped head to pull off the cut. She's over six feet and has the longest legs I've ever seen. Her voice is low, but not too low. It's sexy. I could listen to her talk all night long." Jaime listened to Sarah hum, an indicator she liked what she was hearing.

"Yummy, I like me some tall women. So far so good, go on." Her friend said as Jaime took a breath to continue with her adoration of Austin.

"She has these two sweet little dogs, Clara Jane and Rocky Bob. They are the cutest and well-behaved. You can tell she takes a lot of time with them. And get this, Titus sat on her lap the first night, can you believe it?"

"No way, he sat on her lap? He didn't sit on my lap until you'd been at the park six months."

"I know, right. It's so crazy." There was a pause and then Sarah asked the question Jaime knew she was going to ask.

"What's the catch? What aren't you saying?" Jaime looked at the phone. *How did Sarah know she wasn't telling her everything?*

"Well, here's what's weird. When I took her the cookies, we spent a couple of hours together and made small talk. You know, how long had she been RVing. How long I'd been RVing. The usual stuff you ask someone new in a camp, but to tell you the truth, I've never been so comfortable with someone in my whole life. But the next day, she didn't talk to me -- nor did she talk to me for the next two weeks, in fact, she's been avoiding me. Then today, her Dad and brother arrived at the park and she introduced me to them right away, but as they were warming up to me and me to them, she dismissed me and suggested I probably needed to get back to work. I don't know whether to be hurt or angry," Jaime said looking in the direction of Austin's campsite.

"Wow, Ladybug, it sounds as if you have got quite the situation. I wish I was there so I could watch her. I don't know what to tell ya. I'd give ya a big hug and we could hatch a plan to find out what is going with her, if I was there."

Jaime smiled knowing her friend spoke the truth.

"That's okay, I'm glad I could talk to you about it. I need to figure this one out on my own." They continued their conversation for a few more minutes and then she hung up, as some of her regulars started showing up, perusing books and ordering wine.

A LITTLE COMPETITION

"So, Sis, tell me about Jaime. She's a looker." Junior wiggled his eyebrows at her.

"Is that all you care about Junior? Looks? She happens to be a savvy businesswoman and has the best cat," Austin snapped as she grabbed a beer from the cooler. After their naps, she had shown her Dad and brother around and they were back at her rig having a few beers before they went into town for dinner.

"Whoa there, Austin, if you've got dibs." He raised his hands as if in defense of his words.

"I don't have dibs," Austin said, "but she isn't someone for you fool around with. You're going to be leaving and I don't want to have to deal with your crap that you leave behind." Austin grimaced at her brother as she looked at him. Junior was notorious for his love em' and leave em' ways. Austin couldn't figure out why they fell for his act. Austin had had to pick up more than one girl's heart after her brother was through with them.

"Hey, that's not nice. I don't leave crap, but I may leave some broken hearts." Junior smiled at her and she begrudgingly smiled back. "I'm going to walk over and get some firewood for the fire, want me to pick anything up at the store?" he said. He had noticed the wood pile was low when she showed them around earlier in the day.

"No, we're all set, Thanks. It will be nice to have a fire tonight. I didn't realize I had burned almost the whole pile the last couple of weeks."

Junior looked like her Dad, full of charm and charismatic. He was handsome and full of personality. He was three inches taller than her, with black hair and the same blues eyes that looked back at her in the mirror. He was a successful software developer and was a confirmed bachelor, the only one in the family who had never married. He looked like a model even if he was in his mid-forties. He kept fit by doing all kinds of outdoors sports and if there was such a thing as a modern mountain man, he would fit the bill.

Her other brother was married to wonderful woman whom she loved and adored as well. Dallas, her oldest brother looked more like their Mom. He was six-two, with bright red hair and green eyes. He lived in their hometown not far from her father and helped their Dad out as much as he could. Dallas was quiet and not as outgoing as Junior. She loved spending time with him because they could sit for hours fishing or gazing out at the lake without saying anything to each other. His wife Nancy was the same, quiet and unassuming. They had raised two boys, Carter and Carson, who were going to college in Houston.

Austin loved her nephews and before Maddie died, they would take turns spending the night with them. Once Maddie had passed, they had spent less time with her. She didn't have the energy to deal with two rambunctious boys and her grief as well. Unfortunately, her grief won out. Traveling in the RV hadn't made much of a difference. They were in school and couldn't take off to go camping with her and in the summer, they both had jobs since their parents were firm believers in earning their own way in life. She was hoping with her semi-permanent position at the Purple Cactus, they could come visit more.

Thinking about her family always made her happy and melancholy and reminded her of what she lost when Maddie died. At times, the sadness overwhelmed her, and it was difficult to function. This was one of the many reasons she left home. She needed to get away from the reminders that her family seemed to bring to the forefront every time they got together.

She could take them in small bursts like her Dad and Junior visiting her, but not all of them. She was thankful they seemed to understand her need to be away from them. Her brother and sister-in-law had reassured her that they had explained to the kids that she needed some time. She guessed five years was probably time enough.

During her reverie, she didn't notice her Dad step out of the RV and sit down beside her. "So, tell me about the looker you introduced us to this afternoon." He patted her knee.

"Dad, I swear, you and Junior are cut from the same cloth." She grinned at him. Her Father leaned back in his chair and grinned the trademark Stevens grin.

"She's got her own business, which seems to be doing very well. She's a great baker and from what I've heard a good cook as well. She's so nice, she takes dinner over to Barney, you know the horse rancher, Gus' friend, every Tuesday. She has the best cat Titus, he's part Maine Coon so he's as big as Rocky Bob."

Buckston looked at her in surprise. "That's a lot of information, Sugarplum. I didn't realize you knew her so well."

Austin pondered his statement for a moment. "Well, I don't really know her. I mean I haven't really spent a lot of time talking to her, but I've seen how she is around other people and Barney speaks very highly of her." She leaned forward in her chair and stoked the fire, adding more wood to bring the flames up.

"So why haven't you got to know her, Sis? She seems like a lovely woman, at least she makes a good impression," Junior said as he added a few logs to the pile by the RV.

"I don't know, Junior. I like her, but I can't seem to get past my first week. She came over and brought me cookies. We had a nice time. We made small talk, looked at the stars and watched the fire. I've wanted to talk to her, to really get to know her, but something keeps holding me back. I don't know why." She knew why but didn't want to say it out loud because it would tell them she was still pining away for Maddie, even though she was done grieving. She wanted to move on with her life.

Buckston looked at his daughter for a long time and heaved a big sigh, "Honey, Maddie has been gone for five years. You're young, you deserve to be happy again. Don't hold yourself back because I did. You have a beautiful loving soul, and you should share it with someone."

Austin shook her head at her Dad and said, "Daddy, I'm over fifty for Christ's sake, and I don't even know if she is a lesbian. She has this guy who comes to see her all the time and they look like they are really close." She knew the line was an excuse even as she said it.

"Sis, you can't let that hold you back," Junior added. "You don't know who this guy is to her. You should give her a chance, if getting to know her is what you want." He paused for effect, "Cause if you don't, I'm going to think she is free for me to chase," he said with a wink.

His humor seemed to break up the intensity of the moment and Austin replied with a wink of her own. "You better not Buster, if you know what's good for you." Her comment seemed to lift the heaviness of the discussion and they finished the evening reminiscing about years past.

The next morning Austin arose with a purpose. She was going to have coffee with Jaime. It was time for her to move on.

Barney had given her a list of places to fish and last night before bed, they had decided where they were going to go the next day. Her Dad and brother had left early to check out the fishing at the first place and she was going to join them after she finished her duties at the park, but first things first, she was going to go talk to Jaime.

"Okay, dogs, let's see if we can make a better impression on our friend than we have so far." Both dogs looked at her and bounded to the door ready to start the day and impress their mistress's lady friend. As Austin drew near the bookshop, she saw it was closed, which was odd since Jaime was always open by no later than 7 a.m. There was a note on the door. "Sorry, had to run into town, be back in a while."

"Damnit, I missed her. Oh well, dogs, let's go get our work done so we can go fishin'." She patted her legs and headed off in the direction of the main office.

She slammed the door as she walked into the office. "Hey, Jane, what do we have going on today?"

Jane looked up from behind the desk. "Well, hello, Handsome. It's a light load today. You'll probably be done in a couple of hours." The office manager had flirted with Austin from the beginning and had taken to referring to her as Handsome. She wasn't sure whether she should be flattered or upset about the nickname. She opted for flattered most of the time. Jane was a nice-looking woman

115

and if she wasn't totally devoted to her husband Hank, Austin would have been worried.

"Okay, great. My family is here visitin' and I wanted to meet up with them as soon as I could to do some fishin'."

"Barney give you a list?"

"Sure did."

"Good. He's the best fisherman in the area and knows all the good holes. At least that's what Hank says. I can't abide the damn things. They are so gross and don't get me started on what it's like to clean them. I told Hank if he brings fish home, he's in charge. The only thing I'm willing to do is eat them. I don't even wanna cook 'em."

Austin laughed, "Well, now I know not to bring you any fish I catch."

"You're right there, Handsome. I don't want any. But I bet if you asked Jaime, she'd eat 'em with you," Jane said with a wink.

"Uh, well, uh, I don't know about that" Austin spluttered. Her face turned three shades of red and she reached up to wipe it, hoping to wipe the red away.

"Oh, you are so cute, Handsome. If I'd have met you before Hank, I might have thought about crossing over to the other side."

"Uh . . . I'm gonna go," Austin said as she slammed out the door. She could hear Jane cackling as her fast-paced strides took her away from the office.

~~~~~

Jaime returned to the park around 1 p.m. She had gone into town to replenish her supplies for the bookshop. She picked up a shipment of books at the local post office and went to the store to get more supplies for the hospitality side of her business. She shopped at used bookstores in person and online to keep some of her book costs down. The customers liked the variety of used and new books. She never marked the used books up past five dollars and for the thrifty, that was a good price.

When she would review her inventory and do a cost analysis, a lot of times she found she sold more used than new. However, there were still people who drove the big Class A Rv's and thought buying used was beneath them so she kept an 60/40 balance of used vs. new. There would be another shipment delivered from Amazon, but it wasn't due until late afternoon.

She was halfway through unloading her Jeep when Oscar pulled in next to her and parked. "Hey, special girl, how are you this fine afternoon?" He said as he got out of his car and walked over to her.

He reached into the back and lifted a few boxes out when she said, "I'm fine, why are you in such a good mood?" Jaime said as she grabbed some of the boxes.

"Well, if you must know I have met the man of my dreams and am daydreaming my way into his heart." Oscar looked wistfully toward town.

"Hmm … tell me more, tell me more?" Jaime sang like she was one of the guys from *Grease*. One of her favorite movies. She loved John Travolta and Olivia Newton-John and watched the movie at least once a year. She usually made Oscar watch with her. He would grumble and complain, but she knew he liked it as much as she did.

"I met him last night at the Joker. He was dancing with this floozy of a guy and I knew they were all wrong for each other." He danced around the tables, demonstrating his prowess as a dancer.

"Of course, you did. Did you ask him to dance?" Jaime took an Exacto knife and began cutting open the boxes.

"Well, no, I was going to, but you know a lady doesn't ask a man to dance." He wiggled his eyebrows at her.

She stopped and looked at him, "Do I need to remind you; you are no lady. Chicken maybe, but no lady?"

He laughed and squawked, "No, but he was good-looking and I didn't think he would want to dance with me." Jaime didn't see this side of Oscar often, but when she did, it was because he was really interested in someone. Unfortunately, his choice in men usually equated to a broken heart for Oscar.

"Well, honey, maybe you should go back there and ask him to dance. Maybe he feels the same way and is doing the same thing you do. Avoiding taking a chance," she suggested as she went back to unpacking boxes.

"I do not avoid; I don't want to get hurt again." Oscar grimaced as he took some of the unboxed books and walked toward one of the shelves, gesturing to make sure this is where she wanted the new inventory.

"Honey, it's been seven years and another lifetime since Tim left, don't you think it's time for you to put yourself out there?" She walked over to Oscar and put her arm around his shoulders. Tim had been the first man Oscar had allowed into his heart and although they were good together, Oscar's insecurities broke them apart.

"I put myself out there," Oscar objected without much feeling. He remembered his frustration at himself for not being more secure in his relationship and toward Tim for walking away without fighting very hard for their love.

"I mean really put yourself out there. You have got to trust that you are an amazing person, and someone would be lucky to have you. What can I do?" She hugged him tighter.

"Nothing, your love and support is all I need." Oscar said as he wrapped her in a big hug and gave her a sweet kiss on the lips. Out of the corner of her eye, she sees Austin do an about-face and head in the opposite direction. Jaime closed her eyes and sighs. Timing was everything, and she didn't seem to have it with her Amazon.

Austin walked away from the shop, feeling all kinds of things she hadn't felt in a long time. Jealousy, pain, aching loneliness. The loneliness was always there, but today it seemed to be amplified. She knew something was going on with Jaime and the guy Oscar. She saw the love in both their eyes reminding her so much of how she and Maddie were together. Sweet and loving. She had hoped to see Jaime before she went to find her Dad and brother, but it looked as if she was not going to get to talk to Jaime.

As she headed to her Grand Cherokee, she heard her name, "Austin, hey Austin?"

She turned and walking up behind her was Jaime. "Oh, hey Jaime. It looked like you were busy, and I didn't want to disturb you." Jaime hurried up to stand beside her. She was determined not to let Austin get away again without talking to her.

"You wouldn't have disturbed me; I was talking Oscar off the ledge. He met this guy last night and didn't talk to him, so I was giving him some advice." Austin gave her a startled look.

"Wait, I thought you and Oscar were, you know…"

Jaime broke out laughing. "Oscar and I, no way. He is way too much maintenance for me plus he is on the wrong team for me. I love him, but like a brother." She was taking a chance, she assumed Austin was a lesbian, but you never knew these days. Women were all over the place when it came to preferences and she learned a long time ago not make assumptions. Being direct with someone was her motto in life.

She hated the feeling of being in the dark about the way someone was feeling and especially when she was interested in someone. She had learned in business a person had to stand up for herself and making assumptions about other people was a quick way to get into trouble. One of her bosses taught her to be more direct about the way she was feeling. As she got more experience dealing with people at work, she started being more direct in her personal life. She despised people who played games and she hoped Austin wasn't one of those.

The relief that washed over Austin's face was intriguing to Jaime. *Hmmm... I wonder why she looks so relieved. I didn't even think she really liked me. By the way she's been acting, you'd think I was her least favorite person in the world,* Jaime thought as she waited for Austin to say something.

"Um, well, in that case, I was wondering if you wanted to come over for dinner tonight. My family and I are going to do some fishing this afternoon and I figure we'll catch something and if not, we'll grill something from the freezer. Are you interested?" Austin paused, hoping Jaime didn't see the trepidation she felt at getting no for an answer and then said as an afterthought, "My Daddy thought you were nice and wanted to get to know you a little better."

Jaime looked at her for a few moments as if sizing her up and then said, "Sure, I'd love to. Do you want me to bring anything?"

"No, I've got everything covered." Austin looked at her for a few more moments and as she did Jaime noticed that her eyes turned light blue, almost silver in the sunlight. Jaime sensed a stirring in her body that she hadn't felt in a long time. A wetness at her core and the double-timing of her heartrate; a clear indicator that she was totally turned on.

Austin took her hand and brought it to her mouth and lingered for a moment with her lips pressed to Jaime's skin. Goose bumps broke out on the shopkeeper's arms. She longed to reach out and run her hand over the Amazon's head but didn't want to break the interlude. Austin let go, gave her hand a squeeze and walked away.

DINNER WITH FRIENDS

The rest of the day, Jaime walked around in a stupor. She waited on customers and stocked shelves, but she wasn't there. She was thinking about Austin and what the invitation to dinner meant. And mostly, about what it felt like to be caught up in the older woman's eyes. She couldn't help the constant throbbing at her center, and it was driving crazy. She saw Austin, her Dad and brother return around five in the evening. Austin hadn't told her what time to come over, but she figured by the time she closed the shop and freshened up, it would be time to mosey on over.

The shopkeeper finished her nightly closing ritual and walked to her campsite. She opened the door and Titus was there waiting for her. "Titus, you would not believe what kind of day I've had. I received an invitation for dinner from your favorite person. Yes, that's right, I'm going over to Austin's for dinner. And I'm going to mosey on over, I've really cracked, no one moseys these days. Right,

Titus?" Titus looked her and then the door and let out a yowl.

"Okay, Mister, you can go." She stepped aside and he took off into the evening. *More than likely headed over to Austin's campsite.* A shower was waiting for her and so was relief from the throbbing between her legs. After her rather long shower, she put on fresh clothes. This time, jeans and boots.

She didn't wear boots as often as Austin, but she thought the occasion called for them. She had on a denim blouse with the sleeves rolled up a quarter of the way. She put on her favorite squash-blossom necklace. It was small compared to other ones she'd seen on people, but she loved it because it was the perfect size for her. The stones were turquoise and orange, two of her favorite colors. She topped her look off with a silver cuff and small silver band that had belonged to her grandmother. She spritzed on perfume that smelled like oranges, the only kind she wore, when she wore it. Perfume was not her style, but she was trying to impress the Amazon.

One quick final glance in the mirror she had installed on the door between the bedroom and the rest of the living quarters. She liked looking down the hall at the mirror because it made the place look bigger. She gave herself a wink in the mirror, grabbed a couple of bottles of wine from her built-in wine rack. Another sacrifice she made of closed-door storage. It was a pain when she moved the RV because she had to put all the wine in boxes to keep them from breaking, but once she parked, she loved the look of a wine center.

She turned down the lights and stepped down. It was dusk, so she could still see the path and didn't need a flashlight yet. It would have been difficult carrying a flashlight and two bottles of wine. When invited to someone's home, one didn't show up without anything for the table, at least that was her philosophy, not that she had learned it from anyone, but the sentiment made sense to her.

As she neared Austin's campsite, she heard Buckston talking about the big fish he caught that day and when she looked around a tree, she saw him sitting by the fire, holding Titus and telling the cat all about his day. His conversation with the cat was about the cutest thing she had ever seen, and she knew in the moment, no matter what, she was going to love Austin's family even if nothing came of the attraction she felt for the Amazon.

"You better be careful, Mr. Stevens. Titus might follow you home if you keep regaling him with ideas of big fish. He thinks he a big-game hunter, as it is."

"Don't you worry pretty lady; he knows where his bread is buttered and its Buck to my friends."

"Okay, Buck, where is everyone?" Jaime said as she looked around the campsite. She liked the way Austin had set up her camp and hoped one of these days she might be able to experience a nap in the hammock -- with the Amazon, of course.

"Oh, those two are in the RV getting the fish ready for the grill. We caught three big trout and they have been arguing ever since about the best way to prepare it for cooking. It's an ongoing struggle in our home." He laughed to himself as the RV door swung open and Austin and her brother stepped out.

Austin almost fell out the door, when she saw Jaime talking to her Dad. Her heart began to flutter, and her hands started to tremble. *Oh my God, she is gorgeous. I thought I was going to come undone this afternoon after I kissed her hand, but now . . . Wow, I want to go over to her, throw her over my shoulder and take her to bed. Get it together, Stevens.*

"Come on Sis, what's the hold up? Oh, I see!" Looking past Austin's shoulder, Junior snickered to himself.

Austin regained a semblance of control and said as she stepped down out of the RV, "Daddy, tell

Junior cooking fish without Old Bay is blasphemous and won't be as good."

"Dad tell Austin Old Bay is for steak not fish. Salt and pepper with a little butter or olive oil is the best way to go." They both looked at the patriarch of the family for an answer.

Buckston shook his head at his kids and said, "Well Jaime, what do you think? Who's right?" With a twinkle in his eye, Buckston winked at Jaime.

"Oh no you don't Buck; I'm not getting in the middle of this." Jaime looked at Austin and winked.

"Well kids, I like it either way. Why don't we try both ways on two of the fish and I'll prepare the third fish the way I like it." Buckston grinned at Jaime. She figured he spent a lot of his time while his kids were growing up offering up one compromise after another. The children of Buckston Stevens may have his looks and mannerisms, but his children's interactions indicated to Jaime that both Austin and Junior were very different people.

Austin was more introverted and seemed to take a few moments before she spoke, making sure she said exactly what she intended, or didn't intend to say. Didn't intend to say seemed to be the way Austin approached Jaime. Junior, on the other hand, was extroverted and said whatever he wanted whenever he wanted. This was evidenced by his teasing of Austin and his arguing with her about everything. She had noticed over the last few days when she was watching the Stevens site that Junior and Austin were always arguing about something.

After the fish were prepared, Austin took out a skillet and laid all three fish in it to cook over the open flame of the fire. "This is the best way to cook fish, over an open flame." Austin told Jaime as she laid the skillet on some rocks that had been set up in the middle of the fire.

As the fish cooked, Jaime opened one of the bottles of wine she brought and poured four glasses, "To new friends," Austin toasted as they all clinked glasses. The picnic table was set and there was a nice big tub of potato salad and a pan of baked beans.

The fish cooked quickly, and they all sat down to eat. Jaime took a small section from each fish and loved all the different flavors. When asked, she said she liked them all and didn't say which one was her favorite. Although, she agreed with Junior, olive oil, salt, and pepper were the way she liked to prepare fish.

The talk around the dinner table was mostly about Austin's family. She had another brother who was married and lived close to their Father, just like Junior.

"I think Carter and Carson want to come for a visit this summer," Buckston was saying as they finished up dinner.

"Oh, I'm excited! I love those kids. They are Dallas' kids. I used to spend a lot of time with them before I started traveling and we had so much fun together," Austin said with an expression of obvious devotion.

Junior shook his head and responded, "Your prejudiced Sis, because you know they worship the ground you walk on."

"No, they don't, but they do have great taste in Aunts vs. Uncles." Everybody laughed and the night continued along in that vein. Talk of family and what it was like to grow up with two brothers from Austin and what it was like to grow up with a spoiled sister from Junior.

Toward the end of the evening, the conversation turned to Jaime. "Jaime, tell me a little bit about yourself. Where are your people?" Buckston asked as he took a drink of his wine.

"Daddy!" Austin exclaimed, "Jaime you don't have to tell my family about your 'people'." Austin emphasized her statement with air quotes.

"No worries Austin. I don't have any 'people,' Buck. I was raised in the foster system and never connected with any of the families. My parents were killed by a drunk driver when I was five and my grandmother, who took me in, died from a heart attack a year later. I have Oscar, my best friend, and Barney. I guess they are my people." Everyone was stunned into silence. No one knew what to say. It was foreign to Austin and her family to not have a family.

"Well, I guess on that note, I should be going. Come on Titus." Jaime reached down to pick up Titus and before she could get a good grip, she was wrapped up in a bear hug by Buckston.

"Jaime, I would be honored if you would consider me and my family your people." Jaime was stunned. She barely knew these people but felt good being around them. Something she hadn't experienced in a long time.

"Wow, Buck, I don't know what to say."

"Don't say anything Darlin'. I want you to know that if you ever need anything, you call me, and I'll come runnin'. Well, as fast as, I can get Junior to drive me out here." They all laughed and the attempt at levity seemed to lift the melancholy mood that had fallen over the dinner party.

Jaime started the walk back to her RV in a daze. She had never met a family as loving and giving as Austin's. She didn't know how to react. She has always been on her own. Oscar and Barney were the closest she had to family.

"Hey Jaime!" She turned to see Austin following her. Austin walked up to her and without preamble put her hand on her cheek and said, "My Dad meant what he said and so do I. We would be honored to be your people." She looked in Jaime's eyes, bent down and kissed ever so gently on her lips. Nothing romantic or lustful, but a kiss filled with promise. Jaime stood there for a long time with Austin, forehead to forehead. Not moving, relishing the closeness that one kiss brought them.

"Well, I'll let you go. Is it okay if I stop by for coffee in the morning? My Daddy and brother are leaving early to go fishing again and I've got some stuff to take care of in the morning."

Jaime gave her a big smile. "Sure, I'll be open. Is 6:30 early enough for you?"

"Perfect!" Austin gave her hand another squeeze, turned and walked away.

GOT GUILT

Sometime in the night as Austin slept, she dreamed of Maddie again. *Why are you doing this? Don't forget me. I need you. You're the one I love the most.* Maddie was begging her, beseeching her. Austin was torn up. She didn't know what to do.

But Maddie, you're gone. I need to move on.

Maddie shook her head no. *But you'll forget me, and I'll fade from your memory.*

Austin raised her hand to placate her. *No, no, I won't, I promise. You're my one and only. I love you so much.* Tears trickled down Austin's cheeks as she slept.

Austin awakened overcome with guilt. It was dark in her room and she looked at the clock in the dining room. *4 a.m., too early for me to get up,* she thought.

The overwrought woman tried to go back to sleep, but after another hour of restlessness, she arose. Fortunately, she had a key to the park showers. She loaded up a backpack with her bathroom stuff and headed out to the washroom. She didn't want to disturb her Dad who was sleeping in her bedroom. Her brother had opted to sleep in his truck so she knew she wouldn't bother him with her early rising. She took her time showering, thinking about her dream and the way Jaime looked the previous night.

It's no wonder, I dreamt of Maddie. Jaime is so pretty. I want to get to know her better. Do you hear me Maddie, I love you, but I need to move on! Austin thought as she stepped out of the shower. She approached the fogged-up mirror and wiped at it with her towel. She looked at herself in the mirror and liked what she saw. Her physique was in good shape. She had never had big breasts; they were small and perky. Her work kept the extra fat off and nothing sagged.

"Hmm ... not bad for an old woman," she laughed as she finished drying off. She continued to dress in her standard uniform of late, blue jean cut-offs and one of her many T-shirts. The one she chose to wear that day was of *Charlie's Angels*, one of her favorite TV shows growing up. She loved retro T-shirts and had a bunch. Next came her socks and red cowboy boots. The final accoutrement was her cowboy hat. She took a final look in the mirror and winked.

She could hear the dogs barking as she neared her campsite. It looked as if her Dad had roused himself out of bed to take the dogs out for a walk. She lost her temporary good mood thinking again about her dream.

When she got back, her Dad said, "What's going on honey? Did you have another dream? You're up awful early." The look on her face told him everything. He opened his arms as she entered her home.

"Oh Daddy, I don't know what to do. I loved Maddie so much and I don't want to forget her, but I want to get to know Jaime. What am I going to do?" She looked at him as if he had all the answers.

"Well, Baby girl, Maddie is gone, and you need to let her go. She loved you while she was on this earth, just like you loved her, but there is someone else out there that deserves your love again. Maybe it's Jaime and maybe it's not, but you won't find out if you don't let Maddie go." Buckston pulled her closer and kissed the top of her head.

"I know, Daddy, I loved her so much. It wasn't fair that she left me here." Austin began to sob. She had never cried like this in front of her Daddy or brother. She always did it alone, but she couldn't hold back the tears any longer. As she cried, she felt her brother's arms go around her from the other side and she was wrapped in a cocoon of love from her family.

As her sobs subsided, she looked at Buckston and Junior. She could feel some of the weight lift from her heart. Family was the foundation for her and even though Maddie's death was a chip at her foundation, she still had lots of foundation left. She smiled tremulously at them and kissed them both on the cheek.

"Thanks for loving me and taking care of me. I feel like I don't tell you enough how much I love you both and everyone else in our family. I couldn't have gone on if you all weren't here for me."

"Honeydew, our job as a family is to take care of each other, no thanks needed. But if you insist, I could go for some eggs and bacon for breakfast as a thank you," her Dad joked.

"Okay, you got it. Let me get started on the best breakfast you've ever had." She grinned and moved toward the door of the RV for all the items she needed to make the best breakfast in the world for her two supporters.

~~~~~

Jaime woke up the next morning with a skip in her step. She had never had anyone do or offer what Austin's family offered the night before. She and

Oscar were kids when they met so he didn't count. It was a given, he was part of her family, but having only one person in your corner sometimes wasn't enough. She loved him with all her heart, but she couldn't help but dream of a larger family to love and rely on.

As she took her shower, she thought about the kiss Austin had given her the night before. It was chaste but had a hint of promise. She was excited and fearful at the same time. She knew that Austin had some unresolved issues about a loss, but she didn't know what the loss was and not knowing was bugging her. She didn't think it was her mother because she had died a long time ago. She needed to find out because she knew in her heart that if Austin's angst didn't get resolved, she didn't have a chance with her.

"I'm going to have to talk to her, but not right now. Right now, I think we get to know each other and then tackle the difficult stuff, right, Titus?" Titus turned around and walked toward his bed. "Really, buddy. The least you could do was act like you care." He waved his tail at her and disappeared.

She finished getting dressed and walked over to open her shop for business. 6:30, 7:00, 7:30 rolled around and no Austin. "Dammit, what the hell happened? I was looking forward to spending time with her this morning."

The more Jaime thought about it the angrier she got. "What the hell? I don't think I buy what she said last night. You don't make plans and then not show up. Dammit, Dammit, Dammit!" Jaime walked around the rest of the day with a scowl on her face.

The next morning instead of Austin, she found Junior on her doorstep. "Hello, this is a surprise, how are you this morning?" She smiled at him as she unlocked her shop.

"I'm good. I know it's early, but I would love a cup of coffee if you have one. Dad and Austin are still asleep, and I didn't want to wake them."

"Sure, no problem. Give me a minute to get the coffee ready. Come on in, we can visit for a few minutes." They both walked into the tiny book shop and made their way to the back, where Jaime housed the coffee machine. "What can I get you?"

"Well, I don't go for the frou-frou coffee crap, oops, I'm sorry." Junior looked abashed.

"No apology necessary. I feel the same way, but I've got to meet my customers' expectations, so the cappuccino machine is ready." She laughed as she started making a batch of regular coffee.

"Okay, then. I take my coffee straight up, no sugar." He winked at her and looked around the shop. "You've got a nice place here; I didn't realize you could get so much stuff in here."

"Yes, you'd be surprised. If you are organized enough, which I am, you can get a lot of merchandise in these shelves. Plus, I helped guide the design when the shop was being built."

"You did a mighty fine job. I've never been much of a reader. Austin was always the one who did all the reading, but I like the way you've organized everything and if I was looking for a book, it would be easy for me to find it. I'm more of a podcast or YouTube kind of guy."

"To the detriment of the small bookshop owner. I hear that a lot, but I still seem to do a good business. Maybe it's the venue. With the spotty WIFI connection, people don't have the luxury of watching videos or streaming podcasts."

"My sister said you were a savvy businesswoman and I can see what she means."

Jaime looked at him for a minute and then said, "How does your sister know what kind of woman I am? She seems to be avoiding me."

"Yeah, well, it's not for me to say, but trust me she knows what you are like." He grinned at her as she handed him a cup of coffee.

"I'm sorry. I think I sounded like a real bitch just then. I like your sister and it seems as if we take one step forward and two steps back. I don't know what to do. She is frustrating beyond all get-out."

He took a drink of his coffee and replied, "The only thing I can tell you is to be patient, if you can. She is worth the wait. Think of her as a fine-aged whiskey. You have to sip at her, before you can take a big drink."

She laughed. "Okay, I do like whiskey. Do you have any suggestions for me to move past the sipping?"

He winked at her, "You're going to have to take the bull by the horns and wrestle her down, well, not literally, but you might want to make the first move. She needs a push and I'm thinkin' you're the gal to do it."

"Hmm … you might be right, and I love a good challenge. Thanks Junior, I appreciate your advice." She topped off his coffee and they continued to chat about the park and what living in a RV full-time was like.

Jaime vacillated between being irritated and being exhilarated. Austin never made an appearance, but she knew she was around. She would see the dogs periodically through the trees, but no Austin. Buckston and Junior stayed a couple more days and came by to say goodbye on their way home. She was glad she got to know them and looked forward to when they came back to visit again. Titus still disappeared at night, but she was going to be damned before she walked over there to get him.

A week went by with no Austin. Finally, Jaime had had enough. She marched over to Austin's RV to confront her. Austin was sitting in front of her fire, stroking Titus, big tears rolling down her cheeks. Jaime forgot all about being mad and sat down beside her. She reached over and wrapped Austin in her arms. Austin tried to hold herself back, but couldn't, she fell into Jaime's arms and cried. Jaime held her for what seemed like hours.

Austin finally pulled her head up and looked at Jaime. "I'm so sorry. I wanted to come over to see you, but I couldn't. I'm so messed up and I don't want you to have to deal with my crap."

Jaime looked at her for a moment and then leaned in and kissed her.

The kiss was slow and loving. Just a kiss to let Austin know she was there for her if she wanted her. She stood up, ran her hand along Austin's cheek, picked up Titus, and walked away. She couldn't help Austin. The Amazon had to want her to help.

If walking away meant letting Austin come to her, then so be it.

Austin sat by the fire for much longer than she expected. By the time she roused herself, the fire had gone down and she was ready for bed. She walked the dogs one last time and turned everything off. Once she crawled into bed, she slept like a baby. No dreams, just restful sleep.

She woke up at 6 a.m. and got ready for her day. At 6:30, she walked over to the bookshop and saw Jaime making coffee. She stopped and watched her for a moment. She liked the way she moved. Her morning routine was like a choreographed dance, each movement told a story.

As Jaime started the pot of coffee, she turned and saw Austin standing there.

She walked over to her and waited. Austin looked down into her eyes and wrapped her arm around her waist. Then ever so slowly she kissed her . . . as they stood there the kiss deepened and Jaime could feel Austin's tongue asking to be let in. She opened her mouth and moaned as Austin's tongue plunged into her mouth. They battled each other with their tongues, each trying to take more of the other inside.

The flaring of their passion tried to quench the thirst neither one of them knew needed to be satisfied before their lips met. Austin moved away from Jaime's lips and began kissing her face and slowly made her way down her neck, stopping to nuzzle her earlobe. Jaime could feel the heat rising in her center.

A beeping sounded indicating the coffee was ready. Jaime didn't want to pull away, she had been waiting for a moment like this all her life. The beeping continued interrupting their tableau. "Ohhh ... baby. I don't want you to stop, but I need to check the coffee. Do you want a cup?" Austin pulled away and looked at her with smoldering eyes and stepped back. Jaime felt an instant longing to be back in Austin's arms, feeling her desire for her.

"Sure, I think I need something to distract me." Austin winked at her.

Jaime trembled as she struggled to maintain her composure. All she wanted to do was grab Austin and take her to the back so she could answer the need throbbing between her legs. She grabbed a cup and poured. "Sugar, cream?"

Austin licked her lips as she responded to the barista's question. "No, I take my coffee black. Thanks."

"Just like your brother." Austin raised her eyebrow in question.

"He came over the other day and had coffee. We had a nice chat."

"Really, what did you chat about?"

"You mainly. He told me I needed to take the bull by the horns. Is that what I need to do, take the bull by the horns?" she asked suggestively.

"Oh, I don't know. If I'm the bull, I'm not sure you could handle me." Austin winked at her.

"Oh, I wouldn't count on it. I've been known to wrestle down a wayward bull every now and then." She handed a cup to her. She was about to suggest they repeat their good morning when some of her early-morning customers arrived. Austin gave her a salute and walked back toward her campsite. Jaime stood there for a few minutes running her fingers along her lips.

"Oh, my God, best kiss ever." She looked up to see Barney grinning at her.

"Hey, you ornery old man. Your regular?"

"Yes, ma'am that would be good. I'm going to need it, if I'm going to watch bull wrestlin'," He responded with a smirk. Jaime blushed and turned around to prepare his coffee.

~~~~~

Austin worked hard that day. The park had some grasses and weeds growing up along one of the paths and she had to get them removed before unwelcome guests moved into them. She worked late into the afternoon, trying to expel the pent-up energy brought on by her make-out session with Jaime.

By 7 p.m. that evening, she was exhausted. She walked back to her RV with every intention of going to see Jaime, but as soon as she saw her bed, she lay down for a nap. She woke up from her nap the next day. She took the dogs out and looked to see if the shop was open. *I bet it'll be open once I take my shower.*

By the time she was dressed and ready for another day, the bookshop had opened. As she approached the shop, she saw Jaime talking to her friend Oscar. He was a handsome guy and Austin could see how most people would be attracted to him. As she walked closer, Jaime spotted her and motioned her over.

"Austin, come meet Oscar. Oscar, this is Austin." Austin reached out her hand to shake Oscar's.

"Pleased ta meet ya ma'am!" Oscar said in his best Texas drawl as he shook her hand.

Jaime punched him in the arm and grinned. "Don't mind him. He's a pain. He thinks he's clever and funny."

"Ha. Ha," Oscar said, smirking at her.

"Nice to meet ya, Oscar. Jaime told me a bit about you, but I'm glad to finally put the face to the description so to speak."

"Thanks! Good to finally meet you as well. Are you enjoying working in the park?" he said without any kind of drawl.

"Yes, I am. It's a lot of hard work, but I love it. There's something to be said for getting your hands dirty in the soil." Austin said as she looked at her hands.

"Well, I'm sure there's something, but I'm not sure I agree with you."

Jaime laughed, "Oscar doesn't get dirty. It might mess up his nails."

He held out his hands to show them off, "Hey, manicured nails are important."

Austin stuck her hands in her shorts to hide them from view. "Well, I could probably use a manicure, but it defeats the purpose of digging out weeds and grass like I did yesterday." She grimaced; manicures were not high on her priority list.

"I think you have nice hands." Jaime said and she tugged one of Austin's hands out of her pockets.

"Ah, shucks ma'am!" Austin joked and they all laughed.

They spent a few moments more talking and then Oscar left to head into work. He always stopped in at the bookshop to get coffee before work. The park was out of his way, but the detour was worth it to him to spend a little bit of time with Jaime daily. Plus, he got to finally meet Austin and he could see the attraction for Jaime. *Wow, she is an Amazon!* He marveled at her ability to pull off the almost-bald head. He found the hairdo suited her and even though he didn't know her, he knew she was the one Jaime had been waiting for. He would keep his fingers crossed hoping the two of them figured out that they were meant for each other.

~~~~~

Once Oscar got in his car and drove off, Austin pulled Jaime behind the door in the back of the shop and pressed her body to Jaime's. She looked Jaime in the eye and bent down to kiss her. The kiss was the same as yesterday, starting out slow and gradually becoming more demanding. Austin hands began to roam, taking a slow path down her back to her butt and back up again.

She followed a similar path with her mouth, kissing and nipping Jaime's neck across her shoulders and back up again. Her hands and mouth mimicked each other, memorizing Jaime with taste and smell. The beautiful shopkeeper smelled so good. Her scent was a heady mix of citrus and natural body odor. Jaime's hair smelled like fresh-squeezed lemons and she inhaled the aroma.

Jaime could feel goose bumps rising on her arms and legs like small hills erupting on the surface of the earth. Austin was doing things to her she had only imagined in her dreams. She had never felt so turned on. She returned the touching and tasting. Her tongued warred with Austin's for dominance, both trying to extract as much energy as possible by two lips touching. They kissed and touched for several minutes, each woman basking in the other woman. She wanted to stay like this forever, but she had responsibilities, as did Austin. She was the first to pull away.

"Austin, I, oh, you feel so good. I don't want to stop, but I need to. I've got to get back to work." Austin nipped her earlobe and took in her mouth sucking and chewing. "Austin, oh, my." Her attentions were sending pulses down to Jaime's center.

"Austin, please." She hated to end this make-out session, but she couldn't be responsible for what happened next.

The Amazon pulled away and looked at Jaime with an intensity she had never experienced before. Austin seemed to be memorizing everything about her face; searing her image into her memory. After a moment, she spoke. "You are so beautiful. I can't help myself. I need...." Austin paused, looked down and then back up.

"You're right, what am I thinking? I'm sorry. I shouldn't have taken advantage, please forgive me." Austin moved away from Jaime.

"No, wait Austin, that's not what I meant. I want to continue this, oh you don't know how much I want to continue this, but I've got to get back to the shop." She could see Austin was getting ready to bolt. She grabbed Austin's arm before she could go.

"I am so turned on by you. You are ... oh, I can't even explain how I feel. I want to continue this, please! Can we meet up later after work?" She leaned in to put her forehead against Austin's.

"Please, please, don't go before we make a plan for later." Her eyes were pleading for Austin not to disappear as she had been doing.

"Okay, later, we can get together later." Austin gave her a sweet kiss on the cheek and exited the back room.

Oh my God, my Amazon woman is so hot. I almost lost my dignity. If she would have kept on, I'm not sure I would have stopped. You know what you would have done, you would have begged her to never stop, Jaime thought as she straightened her clothes. She touched her lips and glanced in the mirror she kept in the back room. Her lips were swollen, and she could see that her earlobes were cherry red from Austin's assault. She shivered as she thought about Austin's lips traveling to other parts of her body. She shook her head and walked back out to continue her day.

After work, she went by Austin's RV, but it was dark and there weren't any lights on. She hadn't seen the Amazon leave, but perhaps she was out walking the dogs. She decided to wait. She sat at Austin's site for over two hours, but she never showed.

"Damn her. Damn, damn, damn her." Jaime was beside herself. She knew this was going to happen, she saw it in the woman's eyes before she left. She could see the guilt taking over, but she thought she nipped it in the bud before it took hold. She must have been wrong. Jaime got up and headed back to her place. Titus hadn't shown either, which was her clue Austin wasn't going to be back anytime soon.

Jaime didn't waste any time getting ready for bed. She couldn't decide if she was angry or just frustrated. As she crawled into bed, she thought she would have a difficult time going to sleep, but she drifted off as soon as her head hit the pillow.

Austin pulled back and looked at her, desire in her eyes. Jaime shook her head yes and that was all Austin needed. She lifted Jaime up onto the small counter and pulled her in close. Austin ran her hands up and down Jaime's arms and legs and eventually, worked her hands into Jaime's shorts, unzipping the zipper. She looked at Jaime for permission to go further and the beautiful blonde shook her head yes.

Slowly, Austin inserted her hand into Jaime's lacy panties. As she touched her, she felt the wetness of Jaime's need. She was sopping wet and Austin could feel herself getting just as wet. She slipped her finger into the dampness and ran her callused finger over Jaime's clit. Jaime bucked from the touch.

Austin continued a slow assault of Jaime's clit with her fingers. Moving up and down ever so slowly, never changing the rhythm. All the while, she kissed her mouth, sucking Jaime's tongue in rhythm to the motion of her fingers. As Austin picked up speed, Jaime began moving in rhythm with Austin's fingers. She was moaning and grasping Austin tighter. Austin continued her rhythm, slowly increasing the rate until she was pumping her arm in motion with Jaime's hips.

"I'm so close, please, please go inside me. I need to feel you inside me." Austin entered her with first one finger and then another. "More, I need more!" She slipped in a third finger and continued the rhythm of in and out, plunging faster and faster, while using her thumb to stimulate her clit.

Jaime began pumping her hips faster and bucking against Austin's hand. All the while Austin was running her tongue around Jaime mouth, mimicking her thumb's actions, then she plunged her tongue into Jaime's mouth at the same time she was plunging her fingers into Jaime. Jaime stilled for a moment, hanging in suspended motion not breathing, and then Austin felt the insides of Jaime closing around her fingers.

Jaime moaned Austin's name from the depths of her soul and raised herself off the counter, arching her back and saying, "Oh my God, yes, oh, yes!" Austin held her suspended on the last yes.

Austin continued to kiss Jaime, long after she came down from her orgasm. Loving Jaime felt so good. She missed the act of loving and making love with someone.

Jaime lay there for a moment with her head on Austin's chest, breathing hard. "Oh my, I haven't had an orgasm with so much intensity in I don't know how long. You are so … I don't have words!" She looked at Austin and pulled her close, wrapping her legs around Austin, not wanting to let her go.

Austin heard a noise outside the tiny room, "I have to go, I've got work to do and listening to the sounds coming from the other room you have a customer waiting." Austin slowly pulled her hand loose from Jaime's center and then took her fingers and coated Jaime's mouth.

She leaned in and kissed the beautiful woman's essence away. The Amazon's action was the sexiest thing Jaime had ever seen and she almost came again feeling Austin's tongue licking her mouth, removing any evidence of their lovemaking. Austin stepped away and looked at her and then she was gone.

Jaime opened her eyes and looked around the bedroom. She took a second to wrap her head around what had happened in her dream. She was not one to allow someone to take her, as Austin did. She liked to be the one in charge. Keeping her emotions in check was always the safer way. She had learned early in her life that she needed to be in control of all things, including making love. But Austin was different and had turned her philosophy upside down. Austin had taken her, and Jaime had let her, and she had enjoyed it. Letting Austin make love to her like that was exhilarating and she realized she wanted more.

Jaime wanted Austin to take her for real. She reached down between her legs and her fingers came back sopping wet. She pictured Austin from her dream and her fingers didn't take long for her to bring herself to a real orgasm. She groaned out Austin's name as she climaxed, just as in her dream. She continued to stroke herself bringing about mini orgasms. She exhausted herself and fell back into a peaceful slumber.

THE AMAZON

Austin walked toward her campsite, not believing what she had done. How could she have forgotten about Maddie? She hadn't intended to kiss Jaime, but one thing led to another. She was overwhelmed with the need to feel her lips on Jaime's lips, to feel her as her pulse quickened. She had not felt real desire in so long. Even with Maddie, their kissing had always been gentle, never with unrestrained passion.

I don't understand what came over me. Maybe it's been too long. I've never felt as if I needed to be more physical. I was perfectly happy with the way Maddie and I made love. Maybe I needed to let loose some of my frustrations. She shook her head as she continued to walk, not paying attention to where she was going.

The day was going to be gorgeous. The sky was bright blue, with not a cloud in sight. There was a slight breeze in the air, cooling her as she walked. She could hear cicadas singing and felt as if they were calling to her. Even though she was distracted by her actions with Jaime, nature always seemed to break through to her soul. She strolled along down the path with no destination in mind.

She had not had time to do much exploring of this path, so she set out to see where the route took her. As she walked, she looked ahead, and the path seemed to be pulling her up. She noticed the trees begin to thin out the higher she climbed. Rocks became more prevalent on either side of the path. As she reached the summit, she was overwhelmed at the beauty before her. She could see the striations in the hills creating a multi-color landscape.

There was a naturally flat rock jutting out from the side the hill and she walked over to the outcropping. "Wow, this is a perfect place to sit," Austin said to herself.

She looked out over the gorge and noticed mountain goats climbing up the side of the crevasse. They jumped from rock to rock and she marveled at their agility. Nature was pulling out all the stops for her. As she sat there, she thought about her life with Maddie. Her lover had laid down some ground rules before they officially moved in together and she had readily accepted them. Maddie gave her the feminine stability she had been craving.

Her early life was loving and safe. Maddie helped settle her down and gave her the balance she needed, something she missed after her mother died. She loved her Daddy, but she needed her Mother and when she was taken from her, she didn't know what she was going to do. She was frustrated because she couldn't or wouldn't, if she was honest with herself, talk to her Daddy about everything.

Her frustration led to her acting out. Maddie coming into her life helped her settle down. Maddie was a few years older, and their age difference helped. Maddie had a secure job and was creating a life Austin envied. She wanted security and when Maddie offered safety to her, she took it and grabbed on with her soul.

After Maddie died, she felt the same way she did when her Mother died. She was in an upheaval and didn't know how to handle her chaotic life. She felt like she did when she was a kid. A small boat bereft in a vast sea of pain and misery. Her Dad sending her out in the RV helped her somewhat, though. She was able to create some of her own security, but she was lonely.

She liked having a partner, but the pain was too much to bear. What if she fell in love with Jaime? What if Jaime died too? How was she supposed to let Jaime be in her life, when she missed Maddie so much? These questions swirled around in her head like the maelstrom caused by a whirlpool in the ocean.

Austin didn't know how long she sat there, but the sun was starting to set when she decided to head back down. The hike had taken her a couple of hours to get to the summit so she knew she would be returning long night had fallen. She was going to have to go extra slow because she didn't have a flashlight.

She walked into her campsite after midnight. She could tell someone had been there because her chair had been moved. Jaime must have been here waiting for her. *Stupid, stupid, stupid. I need to apologize to her for not being here tonight. I wonder if she's still up.* Austin walked over to Jaime's sight, but the lights were out. *Dang it, I'll have to go talk to her in the morning.* She turned around and went back to her site, thinking about seeing Jaime in the morning.

~~~~~

The next morning, Jaime started her day like any other day. She opened the door to her shop and started the coffee. She moved the bistro tables and chairs out for the early-morning customers. The club chairs were set out and she straightened the shelves. She was trying to keep herself busy even though she was angry at Austin for standing her up last night; she was also turned on from the dream and her ministrations in the middle of the night.

Her phone rang as she prepared a latte for one of her customers. "Hello, Reading Nook, Jaime speaking."

"Jaime, it's Sarah."

"Hey Sarah, it's awful early for you to be calling. What's up? Are you all right?" She could hear sniffling on the other line.

"My Mama died last night."

"Oh Honey, I'm so sorry. What can I do for you?"

"I know this is a lot to ask, but could you come and be with me?" Jaime could hear the pleading in Sarah's voice. She was too young when her own Mother died for her to know what losing a parent was like but she understood the need not to be alone.

"I sure can. Let me make some arrangements for the bookshop and Titus. I'll be there as soon as I can."

"Okay, text me your flight information and I'll make sure to pick you up at the airport."

"I will, Honey. You take care."

"Okay, thank you." Sarah was trying hard not to break down on the phone.

"No need to thank me. That's what friends are for. I love you, Sweetheart, and I'll be there soon."

Jaime hung up the phone and started thinking about all the things she needed to do before she left town.

Austin had to get right to work the next day, so she couldn't go see Jaime, as she wanted. She hurried through her work orders as quickly as she could and around 2 p.m., she made her way over to the shop. As she stepped into the darkened interior of the bookshop, she could see Jane standing at the register.

"Hey, Jane, what are you doing here? Where's Jaime?"

"Oh, she had to go out of town. Sarah, the park attendant before you, called and her Mama died so Jaime went to be with her."

"Oh my, that's terrible. Did Jaime say when she would be back?" Austin felt like she should feel bad for Jaime's friend, but she was bummed that she wasn't going to be able to see Jaime and apologize to her.

"She figured she'd be gone about a week, give or take a day or two. I'm sitting in for her in the afternoon and I guess her friend Oscar is going to work in the mornings. His hours are flexible where he works." Jane turned to a customer who had come up to pay for a book.

Austin waited for her to finish, "Okay, well, holler if you need me to watch the office or help you here."

"Oh, I'll be okay. I put a note on the office door to come see me over here. Don't you worry, I may be getting old, but I can still juggle two jobs, if I need to," she said with a wink.

"I just bet you can. All right, I'll let you get back to work. See ya later." Austin waved and headed back to her campsite. *Well, damn, a whole week. Shit! Shit! Shit!*

The week dragged by for Austin. She kept herself busy working and even went over to Barney's a couple of afternoons to help him. He was a great guy and she found she liked him more and more as she spent time with him. She also spent time with Oscar. She was driven by boredom and rain one afternoon to hang out at the bookshop with Oscar. She arrived in the shop door soaking wet from a sudden deluge of water.

"Oh my gosh, Amazon, you are soaked." Oscar exclaimed as he rose from one of the bistro tables where he was putting together a puzzle.

"Amazon, uh, what do you mean?" Austin didn't know whether she should be flattered or insulted.

"Oh, yeah. I started calling you Amazon the first time I saw you and the nickname kinda stuck," He said, obviously chagrined.

"Hmm … does Jaime call me Amazon, too?"

He looked at her and winked. "She sure does. She would kill me if she knew I told you."

She grinned, liking the idea of being an Amazon to Jaime. "Okay, we'll keep 'the nickname' a secret then." She used air quotes to emphasize her meaning.

"You better dry off before you catch a cold." She laughed and took the towel he handed her.

"Thanks for the towel. What are you up to this afternoon? I thought you worked the morning shift."

"I do and not much, the rain seems to be keeping customers away. I told Jane I could work all day, since its Saturday."

"Have you talked to Jaime?" She tried to make her interest sound like an offhand comment, but she knew Oscar saw right through her.

"Yes, she called last night. Sarah's Mom's funeral was yesterday. Jaime should be home by Monday." Oscar saw Austin's eyes light up even though she tried to hide her happiness by ducking her head.

"Good, I mean I'm glad she could be there for her friend and I imagine she wants to get home and back to her business."

"I told her she should stay an extra few days just to help Sarah out," he teased.

The horrified look on Austin's face made him burst out laughing. "Just kidding, I'm ready for her to get back, too. I've missed her. He paused, mischief glinting in his eyes. "Have you missed her?"

"No!" Austin exclaimed.

"Hmm ... me thinks the lady doth protest too much."

"I am not."

"You are too."

"No, I'm not."

"Yes, you are." They looked at each other and burst out laughing.

"Okay, maybe I am a bit." She looked at Oscar for a minute, trying to decide if she should ask him the question she had been dying to ask since she walked into the shop. She seemed to make up her mind, with a tiny shake of her head.

"Did she ask about me?" The hopeful look on her face made Oscar smile on the inside. This woman liked his friend and he was so happy. He was hoping Austin and Jaime would get together. He had spent the last few nights on the phone listening to Jaime lament about Austin's lack of interest in her.

"She mentioned you once or twice. I think she was mad at you, but she might be over it by now."

"Yeah, if she was, I deserved it. I've really been struggling. I like Jaime a lot, but I . . ." she stopped.

"You what? Come on, you can trust me." Oscar looked at her waiting for her to answer.

"Gosh, I don't know. You are Jaime's best friend." He could tell she was struggling. She wanted to talk to him, but she also knew if she did, he might tell Jaime and she wasn't ready for Jaime to know.

"Yes, true statement. I am Jaime's best friend, but I would like to be your friend as well. I'll tell you what, when you're ready to talk, you let me know and I'll be here." He could see the relief on her face.

"All right, you got a deal. I better get back to my rig. I left the dogs and they don't love thunderstorms." At that moment, the sky seemed to light up. A fusillade of thunder occurred a few seconds later.

"Okay, see you later, I think I might close up early. Looks like the weather is not going to let up and we'll have rain into the night. I know people won't be venturing out to get a glass of wine or to buy a book." She left him to close the bookshop and ran back to her campsite and two little dogs.

~~~~~

Jaime arrived in Boulder, Colorado a few days before Sarah's mom funeral. She loved Boulder and had been there many times. She especially loved walking up and down Pearl Street looking at the historic storefronts and finding fun new restaurants to try. She figured she wouldn't get much time to do her favorite things but was hoping she could draw Sarah out for a bit. Grief could be all-consuming, and Jaime wanted to help her friend as much as she could.

The day after the funeral, she was able to get Sarah to go for a walk with her. They took Lola along and strolled down the street looking in shops and visiting.

"Jaime, thank you so much for coming to be with me."

"Sarah, you know you can count on me. I wouldn't let you go through this alone." Jaime said as they stopped at a coffee shop for a break. "You want something to drink?"

"A vanilla latte would be great, small. Too much caffeine makes me jittery." Sarah smiled at her, although her eyes remained filled with sadness. Jaime went into the shop and came back out a few minutes later with the requested latte and Chai tea for herself.

"Jaime, can I ask you something?"

"Sure. I've got no secrets." She joked trying to keep the conversation light, knowing she was fighting a losing battle.

"Why did you come? We've never really been close. I tried when I was working at the park, but you always remained at a distance. I wanted to be your friend, but you fought me most of the time. Did I do something to offend you?"

"Oh Sarah, no, you didn't. This is going to sound like a cliché, but it was me, not you. You're one of the sweetest people I know." Jaime paused, trying to decide how to explain. "I haven't allowed myself to get too attached to people. I lost my family when I was very young and moving from one foster-care place to another didn't allow me to get settled into friendships. Oscar and I stayed friends because we went to the same school, but if I had moved far away, I don't think he and I would have stayed friends, either."

"Oh my gosh, how terrible! I don't even know what to say."

"It's okay. There is nothing you can say. Oscar is forever telling me I need to let people in, but I'm so scared. I don't want to lose someone I love, and I've found my life is easier without having a lot of friends." She looked down at her teacup, trying to hide the unshed tears.

"Jaime? Jaime, look at me." Sarah reached over and lifted Jaime's chin. "I'm not going anywhere. I want to be your friend. And I think you want to be my friend, too. I mean acquaintances don't hop on a plane at a moment's notice to come support another acquaintance." Sarah smiled and winked.

Jaime laughed and said, "I guess you're right. Thanks for understanding and being patient with me. I do want to be your friend. No, that's not right. I *am* your friend."

The two women continued their day walking along, talking about anything and everything. And at end of the day as Jaime was closing her eyes to go to sleep, her heart felt full. Full of a newfound friendship brought together by tragedy but ending in a sense of peace.

BACK HOME

Jaime was so happy to be back home. She opened the shop and made coffee, which was a relief from the last few days. The last week and a half had been difficult for her. She wasn't used to being someone's rock. She had kept any friendships at arm's length most of her life except for Oscar. And if she was honest it was because he had come into her life at such a young age, she had not yet learned how to build the barriers needed to stay aloof from people. She and Sarah had worked at the RV park together, but she hadn't considered them more than acquaintances.

Sarah's call had changed the dynamics of their relationship. She could not keep her at arm's length if she had to offer comfort. She was still stunned by dropping everything to fly to Colorado to be with her new friend. Her friend -- the moniker had a nice ring and she was happy to have someone besides Oscar to call a friend, even if she was terrified of the requirements for being said friend.

She had texted Sarah when she got home the previous night, as well as Oscar. Sarah was glad she had made it home without any trouble; thanked her again for coming to be with her; and told her she would talk to her soon. Oscar had said the same thing but added one extra tidbit. Austin had been looking for her and was excited for her to come back.

Having that information swirling around in her head had kept her up half the night, wondering what Austin's interest meant. She was excited and had to remind herself that she was still upset at Austin for standing her up the night before she left. To be fair, she had left, so if Austin had wanted to give her an explanation, she wouldn't have been able to.

They hadn't got around to exchanging cell numbers; however, if she really wanted to apologize to her she could have asked Oscar to call her or text her. Thinking more about the situation, she started to ramp herself up, making herself angrier and angrier. *Damn Austin to hell. She makes me so mad!*

She was slamming things down onto the counter when Austin came strolling in. "Whoa, there, lady, what did the counter ever do to you?" Austin said with a grin.

"Nothing, can I help you?" Jaime did not grin back.

"Brrr … it's a little chilly in here. Should I step out and come back in, maybe the place will warm-up a bit?"

"What do you want, Austin? I've got a lot of catching up to do today and I don't have time to make small talk with you."

"Ooo…kay, I wanted to apologize for not being there the other night. I'm working through some things and unfortunately, you've been receiving the brunt of my inexcusable behavior."

"You're right, your behavior is inexcusable. Why should I accept your apology? You've done this to me several times." The way Jaime was rubbing a cloth in one spot looked as if she were trying to make a hole in her counter.

Stating the obvious, Austin said, "You're gonna put a hole in the counter, if you keep scrubbing like that." Austin reached out and touched her hand to get her to stop.

"Don't touch me. I'm still mad at you." Austin stepped around behind the counter.

"Please don't be mad at me. I was hoping I could persuade you to come over to the rig tonight and have dinner with me. Please, please have dinner with me, I'm so sorry. I really like you Jaime, and I want to get to know you better."

"Well, groveling is nice." Jaime said and raised her head to look at Austin. She knew she had lost the battle as soon as she looked into Austin's eyes. They reminded her of the sky after a morning shower when the clouds had cleared away and all that was left was the vast expanse of blue.

Austin lifted her hand and cupped the slight woman's face, "I am truly sorry, please forgive me?" She leaned in and lightly kissed Jaime on the lips. The gesture was so soft; Jaime wasn't sure she felt the Amazon's lips. She felt another light touch on her lips and arms wrapped around her and pulled her close. A touch of a tongue asking for entry slid across her lips. She allowed the entrance and reveled in the sweetness of the kiss. She felt herself sink into the arms and heard a small groan not realizing it was her own voice.

It had been so long since someone had kissed her with loving intention, she was hesitant to do anything other than enjoy it. The kiss had reached into Jaime's soul and wrapped her up, when Austin lifted her mouth. Jaime's eyes fluttered open and she could see desire and maybe a little bit of something else mixed together in the Amazon's eyes.

"Oh my, I feel lightheaded," was all Jaime could say as she languished in the strong arms holding her in place.

"I hope that's good."

"Oh yes, very good."

"Good, I'm glad. Do you forgive me?"

"Yes, of course I do." Jaime leaned forward and gave Austin a peck on the cheek. She wanted to ask Austin why she was so skittish but opted to not spoil the moment.

"I guess I better get back to work and let you get back to work. I'll see you tonight?" Austin let go of her and stepped back. Jaime felt the absence of the arms the moment they let her go. She wanted to be back in those arms again.

"Yes, what time?"

"How about 7 p.m.? I'll have time to get cleaned up after work and get dinner ready." Austin was looking at her wrist, checking the time making sure she gave herself enough time to get her work done, go to the store and get dinner. Then come back and cook one of her simpler meals. She wanted to give Jaime as much attention as she could, so keeping the meal simple was the way to go.

"Okay, want me to bring anything?"

"How about a nice bottle of red wine?"

"Sure, I've got some good reds I've been dying to try." She paused and looked into Austin's eyes, wanting her to know she was serious. "And Austin,

I would really like to talk about what's going on with you."

Austin's eyes widened. She looked for a moment like a deer caught in headlights and then a look of resignation crossed her face. "All right, fair enough. I'll see you later." She turned and walked out of the bookshop.

Jaime stood there for several minutes running her finger across her lips, watching Austin walk back toward the office. She hoped tonight's conversation would shed some light on Austin's propensity to bolt as soon as they got closer.

~~~~~

Barney was in the middle of mucking out the horse stalls when he heard a "Hello!" from the front of the barn.

"Hey, I'm back here in the stalls." He lifted another shovel full of horse dung and put it in the wheelbarrow.

"Hiya Barney, I got back last night and wanted to stop by to say hello."

"Jaime, I'm glad you're back. How's Sarah doing?" He stopped what he was doing and walked to the front of the stall.

"She's okay. She knew it was only a matter of time for her Momma to be on this earth, but I think she was still surprised."

"Yea, I know what you mean. It's a tough row to hoe when you lose someone you are close to, especially your Momma or your Daddy." Jaime shook her head in agreement and wrinkled her nose.

"Yuck, what's that smell?"

"Horse shit," Barney said with a smirk.

Jaime had been out to his ranch many times but had never been around when he cleaned stalls.

"You want to help me?" He walked to the back of the stall and lifted another shovel full of dung, showing it to her.

"No way, gross! I guess I never realized you had to clean up horse poop. I thought you had someone else do it." She was embarrassed at her own naivete.

"Someone has to do this chore and since I'm shorthanded right now, I volunteered myself. I don't have any help until school gets out, which is a few weeks away. I have two or three local kids who I hire to help me in the summer. It makes it much easier for me to run the ranch during busy season."

"Well, I could come help you if you need me to. I could get Jane to cover for me in the afternoon and come over here for a while."

"No, Honey, thanks for the offer, but I've got a system down and these chores don't take me too long to get done. Besides, don't you have enough distractions?" He winked at her.

"Distractions? What do you mean? I'm doing the same old thing every day."

"Oh, come on now, you can't kid a kidder. I've seen how you look at Austin. Seems like she's distractin' you quite a bit."

Jaime looked at him for a moment and then gave in to sharing her frustration. "Dammit, Barney. She is distracting me. I don't know what I'm going to do with the woman. One minute I think we are finally going to get to know each other and then the next she's made herself scarce and I don't see her for days. I'm so frustrated." She stomped her foot and kicked an imaginary rock out of her way.

"Darlin', have you told her how you feel?"

"Well kind of, but to be fair, she came around and apologized to me this morning about disappearing before I had to go help Sarah. We're having dinner tonight, which is the reason why I came by. I wanted to get a raincheck on our dinner tonight and to check in with you."

"No problem. I've been thinking about trying the new restaurant in town and this gives me a reason to try a new place."

"Oh good, I'm glad this is working out. I love our dinners, but I think I need to make myself available if I want to get any kind of explanation about why she has been acting the way she has."

"And if you want to get the girl." He winked at her. "Absolutely, you should have dinner with her. Would you like a glass of lemonade before you go? I made a fresh batch this morning and I'm about ready for a break." He put the shovel to the side and picked up the handles of the wheelbarrow to steer it out of the stall.

"Yum. I would love some of your lemonade. Is it in the refrigerator?"

"Sure is, I'll meet you on the porch in a minute. I want to dump this last load behind the barn." He turned to wheel out the offending dung as Jaime headed off toward the house.

They sat on the porch for an hour, visiting about her trip to help Sarah and what had been going on at the ranch. He made a decent living running his horse ranch and offering rides into the hills. His age was starting to catch up to him, because it became more difficult each year to keep up with the horses and schedule all the rides.

Barney had been thinking about retiring and selling his business but hadn't pulled the trigger yet. He didn't want to leave Jaime without a good support system. Even though he wasn't her Dad, he loved her as much as a Father does his child. He had been hoping Austin would be the support he wanted for Jaime, but the situation seemed to indicate she was not cooperating. He may have to take some time and have a talk with her.

UNWANTED SURPRISE

Austin worked most of the day guiding people to their sites and helping them get settled in. She spent some time with Jane talking about where she needed to cut grass and pull weeds. Keeping up with the growth of the grass was a never-ending battle. The spring had been a wet one and now they were getting into summer. Nature was blooming and growing, taking advantage of the water provided for the foliage's growth spurt.

She made a quick run into town to the store and picked up items she needed to make spaghetti and meat sauce. She wasn't much of a cook, but she did know how to make a few good things and spaghetti was one of her specialties. Of course, being from Texas she knew how to grill a steak to perfection, but she did like a little bit of variety in her diet, so she occasionally branched out and made something that wasn't on the grill.

She didn't make it from scratch, but she did fancy up the sauce that she bought at the store. She put the sauce in a pan along with some hamburger and Italian sausage. She liked a hearty sauce, so she always added the burger and sausage. She added some chopped onions, mushrooms, yellow squash, zucchini, and carrots. She topped it off with lots of oregano. She always did taste tests while she prepared the sauce and when she was satisfied, she turned the heat down and left it to simmer, while she went and took a shower.

As she showered, she thought about the kiss. Jaime was gorgeous, there were no two ways about it, and she was drawn to her, wanting her with every fiber of her being. Most women who reached the 50-year mark started to show their age, but Jaime still looked like she was in her thirties -- and had the energy of a thirty-year-old as well. To go be with her friend after her mother died had to take an emotional toll and for her to come back and get right back to work without taking any time to recover was amazing to Austin.

The Amazon was lucky Jaime forgave her. She wasn't sure she would and was afraid she had blown it. The kiss seemed to make everything work out in her favor for the moment, but she still had some trepidation around their discussion tonight. Austin didn't know what to tell her. She didn't want to tell her she felt guilty over her dead partner. She'd look like an idiot. She knew she was going to have to tell the truth later tonight, though.

Hopefully, she would be granted a reprieve and they could stick to mundane topics. Maybe she could steer the conversation away from Maddie. *Yeah, right.* Jaime sounded serious about talking tonight and especially talking about why she kept running away, like the coward she was. *I better suck it up and come up with a good excuse. There's no way Jaime will want me if she thinks I'm still in love with my dead partner. Wait, I still love Maddie with all my heart, don't I? Of course, I do. Then why am I worried about what Jaime will think? Man, I gotta get a grip.*

Austin looked at her watch and saw she had time for a quick walk. Walking had proven to be a great way for her to order her thoughts and prepare for any kind of discussion. Since she was going to take a short walk, she left the dogs at home, thinking she didn't want the distraction. She was going to regret her decision.

As she walked, she thought about the kiss with Jaime. Their kisses had been filled with passion, exacting emotions from her, she thought had been buried with Maddie. She thought there might be a hesitation in the way Jaime felt about her. Her disappearing acts didn't help, but she hoped there might have been something else.

Austin figured she was grasping at straws. She knew the hesitation was all her own. She felt guilty there was nothing else to explain the situation between her and Jaime. She reached into her shirt and grabbed onto the ring; she was hoping she would intuit something that would help her reconcile her feelings.

During the time of her marriage to Maddie, she never once considered anyone else. She had given her heart fully and she knew if she was to start a relationship with Jaime, she would need to find room in her heart for the shopkeeper. *Well Austin, you have quite a dilemma. What to do, what to do?* She knew what she needed to do and what she wanted to do.

She gave the ring one more squeeze and lifted the necklace off her neck. She placed the ring and necklace in her shorts pocket. With her mind settled, she turned back to head home and the conversation with Jaime. She hadn't taken more than a few steps when she heard the rattle. The reptile was close, too close.

Austin looked down and realized she had wandered into the tall grass by the stream. It was the same rattler she had seen a few weeks ago except this time the snake was sitting in front of her leg. She had her hiking boots on, so her ankles were protected. She slowly raised her foot to take a step back and the movement caused the snake strike.

The rattler raised itself up into a coil and sprang, not at her ankle but at her upper calf. She felt the fangs enter her leg and she immediately felt icy, burning venom enter her body as pain began shooting through her leg. The snake let go and struck again, biting her in another place on her calf.

After the snake bit her again, she watched as if in a dream as the snake moved away into the grass and closer to the stream. She imagined the reptile saying, "Serves you right, you got in my way and I showed you." She let out a small gasp and laughed at the same time. She was disconcerted to think the snake spoke to her and then she realized the rattler hadn't spoken at all.

She looked down and saw the two bites, small amounts of blood and clear liquid dripping from her wounds. *Probably venom.* Her survival instincts kicked in and she stepped back, stumbling in her haste to get away. She fell backward into the grass. *I hope there aren't any more rattlers around.* She laid there for a few moments. Her leg was already getting numb and was starting to swell.

She knew she had to get help; a rattlesnake bite was not something to respond to slowly. She had read about the types of predators and critters to look out for after she had worked at the park for a few weeks. She wanted to make sure she kept her dogs safe, never thinking the one to worry about was herself. She began crawling toward the path pulling herself along slowly, as the pain was excruciating. She couldn't believe her luck, she was finally at a point where she was ready to talk about Maddie with Jaime and she may be facing death, all because of a stupid snake.

"Dammit, I was so close," she said as she kept pulling herself forward, but her eyesight was beginning to fade. Exerting herself this way was increasing her heartrate which in turn was accelerating the venom through her body. She finally succumbed to the pain and stopped. She shut her eyes thinking she would rest for a minute.

Austin wasn't sure how long she laid there. She must have passed out and knew if she didn't get help, she was going to die. The numbness had reached the upper part of her leg and the pain was pulsating through the rest of her body. Her reading had told her that help had to come within thirty minutes of the bite. There was no way she was going to get help in time, no one knew she was out here. She needed to lie still and slow her heart rate, if she didn't, she would probably die.

Austin could be with Maddie. But was dying what she wanted? Did she really want to leave this life after finding Jaime? She didn't, she still had a life to live and she wanted to continue the adventure with Jaime. She had her two little dogs and her Dad and brother. They needed her. She had to fight for her life, she had to get moving even if her actions caused more damage. No one could see her in the grass, the foliage was too high.

She reached out her hand and pulled herself forward. She could feel the pain moving through her body. She concentrated on not getting excited and put one hand in front of the other, pulling herself along. The numbness of her leg was not helping her move forward, but she had to keep moving.

She tried to sit up and couldn't, she needed to see what her leg looked like. *I can't get up. I hope my leg doesn't look too bad.* She kept pulling herself, but every movement was excruciating. She could feel the sweat trickling down her face and her back. She was also starting to shiver, the effects of the bites, she was sure. She could hear people talking, but they were so far away.

"Keep on moving Stevens, keep on moving!" was her mantra, like the one from that Disney movie. "Keep on swimming, keep on swimming."

She giggled. Now she was getting delirious. "Great, just what I need."

~~~~~

Jaime had hurried home after work and taken a quick shower. She had picked out one of her favorite red blends to go with dinner before she left the shop, so she was ready for their date. She was going to feed Titus, but he was nowhere in sight. "Oh well, you snooze, you lose, buddy."

She walked over to Austin's campsite. There was no movement and it was too quiet. She knocked on the door and heard the dogs bark, which seemed odd to her. Austin usually took the dogs with her when she was left the RV.

Jaime couldn't shake the feeling something was wrong. She still didn't know Austin very well, which was no fault of her own because she was trying, but she did know her routines. Watching from afar tended to lend itself to seeing how people acted in their day-to-day life.

She thought for a second whether it was a good idea to open Austin's door, but the dogs barking gave her permission to open the door. Most people in the park knew each other so Jaime wasn't worried that the door would be locked. She turned the handle and sure enough, it opened.

Both little dogs were sitting in front of the door waiting patiently. "Oh, you sweet babies, where's your mommy? Yum, what's that smell?" She stepped into the small living area of Austin's home and spied the pot sitting on the burner. It smelled so good and she couldn't help but take the spoon and have a bite.

"Oh, this is good, I can't wait to eat it. Where's your Momma?" The two dogs were sitting in the same place they had been when she opened the door. They looked at her as if waiting for permission.

"My goodness, Austin sure has trained you well. Let me turn the stove off, don't want this luscious sauce to burn and we'll go find her. She can't be far if she left you guys here all alone." They bounded out the door not even stopping to wait for her, they ran off down the main path, sniffing the ground as they went.

"Okay, so I guess you guys are on the trail. Slow down, you guys. Don't go too far ahead of me."

She followed behind the two little dogs as they crossed back and forth on the path. They would stop, sniff and then move on. After about twenty minutes on the path, they leapt off the path and into the grass. She followed them and was stopped in her tracks. Austin lay on the ground, arm outstretched as if she were trying to pull herself forward. The dogs were walking all around her, licking her face and licking her leg.

Jaime ran to her and fell to the ground. "Austin, honey, wake up, wake up!" She wasn't moving. She was barely breathing.

"Oh no, not when I just found you. Help! Help!" She rolled Austin over and that's when she saw the bites. Austin's leg was swollen, and her boots were cutting off the circulation to her feet. She wasn't sure what to do. If she took the boots off the poison might move to her feet, but if she didn't then she might lose her foot.

Her thoughts were all over the place. She didn't want to panic but all she could think about was losing Austin. She had never got around to reading about snake bites. People had recommended she understand the predator and critter population, but she didn't like critters and didn't want to read about them. She had read about the body and how circulation worked so she decided to take the boots off.

"Help, help, someone please help." She yelled as she tried to make her Amazon comfortable. The dogs instinctively knew she was trying to help so they stayed out of her way by sitting on either side of Austin's head.

Jaime's panic finally got the better of her and she began to cry. Her mind froze for a moment, then one of the dogs licked her hand and brought her back to the moment. She rubbed her legs trying to decide what to do, when she felt her phone. She pulled the I-Phone out of her pocket and dialed Barney's number. The phone rang several times, but he didn't pick up. She hung up and tried again, still no answer.

"Dammit, Barney, where are you? I need you; I don't know what to do."

Jaime looked at her phone thinking about who else to call and dialed Oscar's number. He was in town, but at least he could send an ambulance. The phone rang twice and he picked up.

"Hey, beautiful what a nice surprise."

"Oh, Oscar, I need your help." There was a deep sob from Jaime.

"James, what is it, tell me?"

"It's Austin, she's been hurt, looks like a rattle snake. I don't know what to do. I knew we had those things around here, but it never dawned on me that someone might get hurt, especially Austin, she is so strong and sure. I don't know what to do." She was rambling and she knew it, but she couldn't seem to stop, maybe if she kept talking, she would wake up from this terrible nightmare.

"James, Jaime, calm down. Pay attention to me, is she breathing?" Jaime leaned over to look at her chest, it was moving.

"Yes, but barely. Her breaths are coming in shallow gasps." Jaime was finding it difficult to breathe as well.

"Okay, listen, I need to hang up and call an ambulance."

"No, don't leave me, please!" Jaime was gasping and crying at the same time. Oscar wasn't sure whether she was talking to him or Austin.

"Jaime, I need to, or Austin will die. Her breathing is not good, and we need to get her help as soon as we can. Take a couple of deep breaths for me."

Jaime took a breath and then another, which seemed to settle her down. "Okay, what do I do?"

Oscar didn't speak for a moment as he was trying to remember his snakebite training, he never thought he would need the training, but some guy he had dated took him along to first-aid class. He was thanking the guy right now, but at the time he thought he was lame for taking him on a date to a first aid class.

"Keep her head level with her feet, do not elevate them. Does she have any constricting clothes on? If she does, loosen them. Once you've checked her out, sit tight and make her comfortable." Jaime was glad she had removed Austin's boots.

"Okay, call me back after you call the ambulance." She took her friend's head and placed it flat on the ground.

"Okay, I will, Sugar. Don't worry, these guys around here know what to do. I'm going to call and then get in the car to come to you. I'll call you as soon as I get on the road."

"Okay, thank you." Jaime hung up the phone and let the dogs put their heads in her lap and they all sat there. Jaime was praying Austin would be okay and the two little dogs were licking first Austin's face, then Jaime's hand as she stroked the Amazon's brow.

The ambulance arrived within fifteen minutes after Oscar called. They asked Jaime to move aside, but she didn't want to leave Austin. "Ma'am, we need you to move."

Oscar walked up as they were trying to get to Austin. "Come on Jaime, help me get Austin's dogs. We need to get them sorted out and the paramedics need to take care of Austin."

Jaime looked up at him and finally shook her head okay. She let him lift her up out of the way. The paramedics went right to work. Jaime watched them as they worked. She didn't know what she would do if Austin died. Oscar wrapped his arm around her and held her while she watched. The two little dogs sat down beside Jaime knowing there was nothing they could do to help but be there for their mistresses' friend.

IT'S OKAY TO LOVE AGAIN

"Austin, Austin, Honey, wake up!" Austin heard the voice and tried to open her eyes, but she couldn't get them to open.

"Come on, baby, wake up." She tried again and finally, they opened into slits. It was so bright; she couldn't see anything. She shut her eyes again, but then tried to open them a little further.

"That's right, baby open your eyes." Austin struggled to open her eyes, she wanted to keep her eyes closed a little longer, but her partner was waiting for her.

After a moment, she opened her eyes and focused, "Maddie, what are you doing here?"

The woman she had loved for so long was looking at her with a loving expression and was stroking her face. "I'm here for you, Sweetheart. You needed me, so here I am."

Austin had a puzzled expression on her face, "I don't understand. You're gone, how can you be here with me?"

Maddie's expression changed to one of concern. "Oh darlin', don't you remember? You had a run-in with a rattler. You're barely alive. You're close to coming to be with me and I'm here to help you. You have to decide, do you want to stay, or do you want to go?"

Austin looked at her with questions in her eyes. "What do you mean? Of course, I want to stay, I want to stay with you. I need you and I miss you so much." The answers came so easy, but the question remained, did she love Maddie like she used to before her loving partner left her?

"Do you really, Sweetheart? Look into your heart . . . what is your heart saying?" Austin continued to look at Maddie pleading.

"Yes, I know it is."

Maddie shook her head, "Oh baby, think about it." Austin didn't know why Maddie was acting this way. Of course, she wanted to be with her, she was her one and only. The person she was going to spend the rest of her life with or at least the plan had been for them to be together forever.

"What about Jaime?" Maddie was looking at her with acceptance shining in her eyes.

"My love, what do you mean? I love you!" Austin panicked. Maddie was starting to fade.

"I know you love me, and I'll always love you, but Honey, what about Jaime?" Austin struggled with what was in her heart.

"Oh Maddie, I don't know. I don't know what to do. I feel so different with her than I did with you. I'm not sure I want different." Austin continued to look at Maddie. She had loved this woman so much. She knew every curve of her face, every inch of her body. She was safe and happy with Maddie. They got along so well from the very beginning. And with Jaime all she felt was chaos and upheaval, Jaime was always mad at her. Well, if she were truthful, she was at fault for Jaime's ire.

The petite blonde had a passion simmering beneath the surface. Austin knew she was going to take her to the next level of loving. Jaime made her want to do things she had never ever considered doing with Maddie. She was dangerous, making her feel things she was scared to feel. She was being sucked into a maelstrom of emotion, something she had avoided most of her life. The reason she had married Maddie was that Maddie was calm and settled her down. Jaime made her want to let loose. And the feelings terrified her.

"I don't know what to do, Maddie, I'm so scared. I liked our life together; we had a simple and safe life." Maddie continued to fade.

"I know, Honey, and our life was a great but maybe it's time you mixed things up a bit. I like this Jaime. She has you feeling things you never felt before even with me, which for the record is okay. It's time for you to let me go. Go live your life, be with Jaime."

Austin started crying, knowing her love was right. "Maddie, I love you and I don't want to lose you again." Maddie was continuing to fade, but Austin could still see her.

"Sweetheart, you are never going to lose me. I will always be right here in your heart." Maddie placed her hand over Austin's heart and all the sudden, Austin bucked and felt a jolt through her whole body. The pain was excruciating.

"Wait Maddie, I need a few more minutes." Maddie had faded almost completely.

"Goodbye, my Austin, I love you!" Another jolt and Maddie faded away and another jolt and Austin felt overwhelming pain as she gasped for breath.

"We've got her back. Let's get her on the gurney and get her transported." Austin was lifted into the air and she felt herself rocking as if she was being carried. She felt her hand enclosed in another and she opened her eyes to see Jaime looking down at her. Tears were rolling down her face.

"You're going to be okay; I mean you better be okay or I'm going to be mad at you." Jaime leaned down and kissed her forehead. Austin shut her eyes and knew she would be okay. She didn't want Jaime to be mad at her anymore.

"Thank you, Maddie. I love you and will never forget. Thank you for giving me Jaime." She felt a brief whisper of a kiss and knew Maddie was there with her.

~~~~~

They rushed Austin to the local hospital. Oscar and Jaime followed close behind the ambulance. Once they arrived, the waiting game started. The doctors rushed the Amazon into an emergency room but wouldn't allow Jaime to go any further with her. She had heard the paramedics say she had arrested twice on the way to the hospital. She didn't know what she would do if she lost Austin.

Finally, after four hours of waiting, the attending doctor came out to talk to them. Barney had arrived not long after the medical staff took Austin, so they all rose from the waiting room chairs when the doctor appeared. Jaime couldn't tell how Austin was doing by his expression.

"How is she? Is she going to be okay?" Jaime was close to losing it.

"Are you Jaime?"

"Yes, how did you know?"

The doctor looked at her for a moment and she knew the news wasn't going to be good. She felt her legs give out as Oscar and Barney supported her.

Barney looked at him with a thunderous expression. "Doctor, you better tell us what's going on right now." The irritated man threatened an "or else" in his voice.

"Oh sorry, I'm so sorry."

"Oh no, no, no!" Jaime cried.

"It's okay, Honey. We're here for you." Oscar exclaimed as he took Jaime in his arms.

"Doctor, when did she die? I need to call her family and let them know," Barney said sadly.

"Oh, my goodness, she didn't die. We thought we lost her a few times, but she's a strong one. Every time she came to, she would ask for Jaime." They all looked at him like he had two heads.

"I-ah-oh shoot. I'm sorry. I should have said she was okay right away."

"Yes, you should have," Oscar said vehemently. If Oscar hadn't curbed his violent streak a long time ago, he would have popped the guy in the nose.

"She has a long recovery period ahead of her, but the swelling is starting to go down in her leg since we administered the rattle-snake Antivenom.

Her heart rate is still a little fast for comfort, so we are keeping a close eye on her. She's been moved to I.C.U. and you should be able to see her in a couple of hours," the doctor said hurriedly. He knew he had messed this up and couldn't wait to get away from these people. The little blonde looked like she was going to rip his heart out.

"Thank you, doctor. Where is the intensive care unit?" Jaime said with no warmth whatsoever in her voice.

"It's down the hall to the right. Just follow the blue lines on the floor," he stuttered as he turned to flee the obvious murderous intent of the sick woman's friends.

When they arrived in the I.C.U., the nurse directed them to the waiting room and said she would let them know when they could see Austin.

"Honey, are you okay? I'm so sorry that doctor was such an ass," Oscar said as he took her hand.

"Do you want me to speak to management about him? I will if you want me to," Barney said as he took her other hand.

Jaime sighed, coming down off her emotional high. "No, that's okay. I'm just glad Austin is going to be all right. I should call her Dad and let him know what happened."

"I'll do it. Do you have his number?" Oscar offered.

"Yes, the number is in my phone." She took her phone out of her pocket and held the front to her face. As soon as the screen opened, she handed him her phone and sat back in her chair, finally feeling the pressure of the afternoon release. She had been so scared. To know Austin was going to be okay was a welcome relief from the alternative she had been thinking was going to happen.

"Ma'am. You can go in, but only one at a time," the nurse said as she stood in the doorway of the waiting room.

"You go on ahead, Sweetheart. We'll be right here," Barney said as he squeezed her hand.

Jaime got up and walked with the nurse to where Austin was sleeping. Jaime gasped as she walked up to her Amazon's bed. She had tubes coming from everywhere. There was a machine beeping in the background with a steady rhythm of peaks showing her heartbeat.

She was afraid to touch her, but she needed to touch her. She reached out with trembling fingers and caressed her face. Austin looked peaceful even though she had a tube coming out of her mouth.

Jaime leaned down and spoke in her ear. "You're going to be okay, Sweetheart. I'm right here. I'm not going to leave you, so you sleep and get better. Okay?"

The beeping continued, giving Jaime a sense of comfort. She was glad Austin was the only one in the room. Hospitals were bad enough with the smell and all the sick people. Jaime wanted Austin to get better and having sick people around was a recipe for disaster as far as the bookshop owner was concerned.

The nurse came back into the room and said, "She should only be in here for about twenty-four hours. She's reacting well to the medicine and should be in a room tomorrow night. Unfortunately, I can't let you stay much longer."

"Oh, okay. Just a few more minutes, okay?"

"Sure, I'll give you five and then you are going to need to go."

"I don't have much time, baby. I'm going to have to leave you for a while, but you can rest assured, I'll be back tomorrow, and I won't leave your side until you're ready to leave this hospital. And don't worry about the dogs. I'll make sure they are taken care of until you get better." Jaime continued to caress Austin's face and when it was time for her to go, she leaned down and gave her a kiss on the lips, not caring about the tube.

She walked back into the waiting room and Oscar said, "I talked to her Dad. He and the brother, Junior, are leaving tonight. Should be here tomorrow evening."

"Thanks, honey. I appreciate your calling him. His arrival will be perfectly timed because Austin should be out of I.C.U. by tomorrow night."

"What do you need, darlin?" Barney asked as he pulled her into a hug.

"I'm okay Barney. I could use a ride home. I need to take care of her dogs and Titus. Put some clothes together for her. And Oscar, could you and Jane handle the shop for a while? I'm planning on being here when she wakes up."

"Absolutely, don't you worry about a thing. Let's get you home so you can come back in the morning." They all walked out of the waiting room and Jaime looked back once more at the room where Austin was sleeping -- and healing.

~~~~~

The next few days went by in a blur for Jaime. Austin was moved to a private room and her Father arrived by the following evening. Austin had remained unresponsive, they had taken the breathing tube out, but she had not awakened. The doctor assured both Jaime and Buckston this was not unexpected, and he thought she would wake up in a day or two. Her body was healing and needed to rest for her to get better. Jaime was skeptical and didn't trust him, only because the doctor hadn't won any points with her when he led her to believe, if only for a moment, that she had lost Austin for good.

On the fourth day, she was sitting by Austin's bedside, holding her hand and had dozed off. Buck was in the room as well and when he looked over at his daughter, her eyes were open, and she was looking down at her hand grasped in Jaime's.

"She's been here the whole time you've been here, darlin'," he whispered to Austin when she looked at him with a question in her eyes. "I've been hard-pressed to get this little gal to leave you alone for a minute. She's barely left to go home and shower. I know she's exhausted, but she refused to leave you."

With a scratchy voice Austin said, "She's a keeper. I'm sorry it took me so long to figure it out."

"Don't you worry, Honey. I think she has every intention of getting you lined out." Buckston chuckled and caressed her cheek.

"Could I get a drink of water? My throat is so dry and I'm thirsty."

"Coming right up." Buckston reached over to get her some water and slipped the straw in her mouth. "Take it easy. Not too much." Jaime opened her eyes. Those were the most beautiful eyes Austin had ever seen.

"Hey you, you're awake." She leaned over and kissed Austin on the forehead.

Austin closed her eyes and relished the affection she felt for and from the little shopkeeper. "You gave us quite a scare. I haven't decided whether I'm mad at you or relieved." Jaime said sternly.

"Please don't be mad at me. I know I've been a pain in the ass, but I really wanted to talk to you the other night except for you know, the whole wrestling with a rattlesnake," Austin joked.

"Not funny, Amazon." Jaime looked at her with a frown.

"Well, I think that's my cue. I'll go find Austin's brother and bring back a cup of coffee or a bottle of water?"

"Coffee would be great, thanks Buck. You know how I like it," Jaime said as she looked at Austin, not wanting to let her out of her eyesight. Buckston blew his daughter a kiss and closed the door.

"I really am sorry. I know we need to talk, but I'm really tired and was hoping we could do it a little later."

"You're lucky. I'm a forgiving woman and am willing to have this talk another time," Jaime said as she leaned over and kissed Austin on the lips. The Amazon loved the feel of the shopkeepers' lips on hers. She would have loved to deepen the kiss, but she didn't have the energy.

Jaime lifted her head and looked into Austin's eyes. "Hey."

"Hey back."

"Go back to sleep, I'll be here when you wake up." Austin closed her eyes and relaxed, knowing Jaime was no longer mad at her. She had found someone who she was going to love for the rest of her life. . . .

Once Austin was out of the woods. Jaime stopped sleeping overnight at the hospital. She moved into Austin's place to take care of the dogs, which meant Titus moved in as well. She loved sleeping where Austin slept. She felt close to Austin, smelling her fragrance on her pillows. The aroma was an earthy smell with a hint of lavender. Most likely from her shampoo, which Jaime had discovered the first time she took a shower in Austin's RV.

She was traveling back and forth to the hospital, but knew she needed to get back to running her business. Her customers understood, but she was getting restless sitting around the hospital. Austin was recuperating well and would be coming home in the next day or so. Jaime couldn't wait to get her home. Home was going to be where Austin lived. She knew in her heart that the Amazon was the one.

Austin's Dad and brothers had come out the first week and everyone had taken turns staying with her and Jaime. Buckston had been right, she was accepted into the family, no questions asked, and when it came to Austin's care, Buckston deferred to Jaime even if she and Austin weren't officially a couple.

Everyone had been nice to her, and she especially liked the wife of Dallas. She thought it was kind of quirky that their kids were named after Texas counties, but it seemed to be a tradition with the family since Dallas had named his boys Carter and Carson. They were counties she had never heard of. She had to look them up on a map.

Barney and Oscar had been part of the parade of caretakers as well. Each one had spent a little time with Austin, talking with her, even in those first couple of days when the Amazon was lying in an induced coma. The doctor had wanted her to heal properly and felt the coma was the best treatment, as Austin was constantly stirring around from the anti-venom that was used to help her get better.

Her body had reacted differently from that of most patients.

The doctor wasn't sure what caused her reaction -- whether her response was an allergic reaction, or she had been close to death when the medicine had been given to her. He had told everyone the best thing for Austin was to put her in a coma and let the medicine do the work while she was calm. He also recommended they talk to her, reminding Austin there were people waiting for her.

~~~~~

One evening when Barney was watching over her, he took the opportunity to have his talk with her. He felt he could say what he wanted without worrying about hurting her feelings.

"Well, Lady, you have caused quite a ruckus for all of us, but especially for Jaime. That little girl doesn't know it yet, but she loves you. I can tell by the way she looks at you and the way she talks about you. But you need to know, you are frustratin' the hell out of her. Excuse my language." He paused for a moment to take drink of water. He usually didn't talk this much.

"She needs you and I think you need her, too. I don't know much about what happened with you and I don't think I need to know, but you better tell my little girl. My little girl, she may not be mine by birth, but she is mine by love and I love her. If you're not going to do right by her, then you need to move on. She needs someone who cares about her and wants to make her happy." He took her hand in his, marveling that for a tall woman, she had small hands.

"I like you, Austin, and I'm sorry if what I say offends you. I needed to say it and I know you can hear me. I figured this would be easier for both of us, if I caught you with your pants down, so to speak." He laughed at his comment. And even though he wasn't sure, he thought he felt her hand squeeze his. He continued to hold her hand for the rest of the evening.

The days went by quickly and once Austin woke from her coma, she improved quickly. The family stayed as long as they could, but eventually, they had to get back to their own lives and the family business. They all left slowly over a couple of days.

Buckston and Junior were the last to leave. Buckston pulled Jaime aside before they left, and she would never forget their conversation.

"Jaime, honey, do you have a moment to talk?" They had stepped out of Austin's room so she could rest, and Junior was heading off to get the truck to drive home.

"Sure, Buckston, want to talk in the waiting room?"

"No, let's go outside. You can walk this old man to Junior's truck." He gestured to the elevator and the way out.

"You're not old, Buck. You're the youngest old guy I know," she teased. They walked toward the elevator and got on.

"Jaime, I want you to know how much I appreciate all you've done for Austin. You saved her life and I am eternally grateful."

She looked at Buckston with a self-depreciating smile. "Oh heck, it was no big deal. I'm glad I found her, but to be honest I was a mess. Oscar's the one you should be thanking. He's the one who called the ambulance."

Buckston pursed his lips and said, "I'm not talking about the logistics little girl, I'm talking about your saving Austin. She was alone for a long time, and it was by her choosing I know, but you saved her." Jaime looked at him as the elevator doors opened and he held his arm out for her to proceed him out.

"I don't think I know what you mean." She took his arm as he looked down at her.

"I mean, you saved her from herself. She had been struggling for several years after her partner,

Maddie, died. It was hard on all of us. We all loved her so much and she was good to and for Austin." He looked at Jaime, trying to get her to hear what he was saying.

"You see, Austin was a restless child when she was younger. Always getting into trouble and to be honest, I didn't know what to do. I sent her off to college hoping she would settle down, but her impatience with life seemed to get worse. She partied all the time and didn't seem to spend any time in class.

To this day, I don't know how she got her degree, but she did. She was offered lots of jobs when she got out of school, but she didn't want to do anything. She lounged around all day and went out partying at night. I was at my wit's end -- and then things changed." He took a breath and continued.

"She started looking for a job and she stopped going out at night. I was dumbfounded. I didn't know what was going on. I found out when she brought Maddie home to meet the family, I knew she was the reason. She settled Austin down. It was like a light went off in Austin and she became this loving, happy member of my family. Her brothers were over the moon for Maddie and to be honest so was I. She saved Austin." Jaime looked at him with sadness in her eyes. Was this his way of telling her, he appreciated her help with Austin, but Maddie was always going to be number one in his eyes?

"I see what you're thinkin' and you've got it all wrong, little lady. You are the next step in Austin's evolution. Maddie grounded her when she needed to be grounded, but you've set her free. She can fly with you. You ignited a passion in my girl, a feeling I haven't seen before. The way she looks at you makes me blush. She never looked at Maddie that way." He paused thinking about his next words. He wanted to get them right.

"Don't get me wrong I know she loved Maddie with her whole heart, but you've ignited her passion and I'm so happy she can finally be balanced. I want my fiery girl back, the one who wasn't afraid to do her own thing. She needs you and so when I say you saved her, you saved her." Jaime was dumbfounded at his heartfelt story. She had only been following her heart -- the Amazon moved her. Igniting Austin's passion? She wasn't sure she believed she could cause a change like Buckston was describing.

"Buck, I don't know what to say. Thank you for telling me about Maddie. I didn't know much about Austin's life before the park. We hadn't had time to talk about how she was feeling before the accident.

Now, I understand why she avoided me so much and trust me, we will have words."

Buckston chuckled to himself. *Oh no, Baby girl, you've got your hands full with this one.* He put his arm around Jaime, and they walked quietly to his truck. Both enjoyed the feeling of knowing Austin was going to be okay.

GOING HOME

Austin lay in the hospital bed for a long time, thinking about Jaime and what she wanted to do to her when she finally got out of the hospital. Her leg was healing, and she still felt weak, but she felt sure she could take care of Jaime's needs. As she thought about what a passionate night with Jaime would be like, she began to feel herself get wet. She imagined her tongue running up and down Jaime's body, suckling her breasts, one right after the other, driving Jaime wild.

She imagined her hand slowly making its way down Jaime's stomach and over her hips. As she lay there, she felt her own hand reach between her legs and tweak her clit. She bucked off the mattress and grimaced in pain, putting a strain on her healing leg. Her heart rate sped up and she felt the wetness seep out from her center to run down her legs. She reached in with hand and ran her fingers within her folds, moving up and down, never touching her clit but running alongside it.

She imagined Jaime kissing her and she moved her fingers to her clit, stroking her engorged nub as she reached the pinnacle of her desire, she pictured Jaime above her offering her a taste and the thought of this most intimate act sent her over the edge. She came down slowly from her high and eventually fell into a deep, dreamless sleep.

The Amazon awoke with a start. She had only been sleeping for about thirty minutes, but it felt as if she had been sleeping for the last five years. She looked out the window and could see her Dad and Jaime walking to his truck arm in arm. Junior was waiting in the driver's seat. She smiled to herself, if her Dad and Junior liked Jaime, hell if her whole family liked the petite shopkeeper, then all she had to do was convince Jaime she was the one for her.

Jaime had been nice to look after her, but she had a business and people to look after, like Barney and Oscar. She didn't need someone else to look after not when Austin was perfectly capable of looking after herself. She lay there for a while thinking about her life and Maddie, when she heard the door open. Jaime looked in, saw she was awake, and walked on in.

"Hey, you, how are you feeling? You're supposed to be napping." Jaime walked over to the bed and began rubbing Austin's arm.

"I couldn't sleep. What were you and my Dad talking about? You looked so intense."

"Oh, you and me and you know, stuff." Jaime avoided eye contact with her. Now was not the time to get into a conversation about her dead partner.

"Stuff, huh, anything interesting?" Jaime turned and looked at the door, cutting the conversation off.

"Nope, has the doctor come by?" Austin touched her arm so she would look at her, "Yes, he says I can go home tomorrow."

"Wonderful news, I'll get my stuff out of your place." Jaime busied her hands with fluffing Austin's pillow.

"You don't have to, I mean, if you don't want, I might need some help in the night, and I'll feel better knowing I'll have help, of course, only if you want to stay." Jaime looked at her for a moment.

"Are you sure? I mean, I don't mind staying and helping, but I don't want to intrude on your recovery time and especially your time with the dogs. They really missed you."

"No, I'm sure, it will be great having you there and I'm sure the dogs will want you there as well. What about Titus?" Austin couldn't resist, she let her fingers glide across Jaime's arms.

"Ah, well . . ." Jaime looked at her sheepishly. "Titus has been staying there as well, but I'll take him home." Austin continued to caress Jaime's arm, raising goosebumps.

"No way, you stay, the cat stays, besides I've grown fond of the big fella." Jaime shifted and Austin's hand fell away. Jaime noticed the absence immediately.

"Okay, well how about I pick you up in the morning, get you home and settled, and then I'll make a nice meal tomorrow night." She wanted Austin to keep caressing her, but there was no way for the Amazon to continue without Jaime being obvious about wanting her touch.

"Tomorrow is Tuesday, right? Don't you need to go over to Barney's?" Jaime clasped Austin's hand in her own, wanting to feel her touch.

"No, I've already made arrangements to go over on Friday. Maybe if you're up for it, you could go, too." Austin looked at their intertwined hands and smiled.

"Sounds like fun, let's see how I'm feeling. My leg is still weak and it's a bit of a struggle to walk some days." She grimaced, because she hated not to be able to move around like she wanted to.

"I know, Sugar, you let me know what works for you." Austin preened at the endearment and held Jaime's hand tighter. They sat for a few more minutes and as much as Jaime didn't want to leave, she needed to get back to her shop. Jaime kissed her on the forehead, said goodbye, and headed back to the park.

When Jaime returned to her shop, Oscar was waiting on a customer. As soon as he finished, she said, "Hey, how's it going to today?"

"Excellent, my lady, you are making a killing. I've been busy all afternoon. How's our patient?"

"She's good, the doctor says she can come home tomorrow. I'm going to pick her up in the morning." She kept her attention on the customers.

"Whoa, ho, are you are avoiding looking at me? What's going on?"

"Oh Oscar, I don't know if I'm ready for this. I like Austin a lot, but her Dad told me why she has been avoiding me. Her partner died. I mean what am I supposed to do? How am I supposed to act? I can't compete with a ghost." Oscar made his way over to her and pulled her into a hug.

"Hold on there. Don't you think you are putting the cart before the horse? You need to talk to Austin about what you are feeling. You can't make these kinds of assumptions. I know you're scared, but Honey, I know Austin means more to you than just 'like'. I've seen how you look at her especially when you think no one is watching."

"What do you mean how I look at her?"

"Oh, don't be coy. You've got it bad for the Amazon." He grinned at her.

She looked at him, ready to deny it, and then shrugged. "It's that obvious?"

"Yes, ma'am, Barney even noticed. He told me he had a long talk with her and let her know that she better make up her mind what she wanted, because he wasn't going to put up with someone playing with his little girl."

"Barney said that?" she asked with wonder in her voice.

"Yes, he did. You know he loves you like a daughter and I applaud him for taking the steps necessary to make sure you're happy."

"Wow, I don't know what to say." Tears began to run down her face. Oscar pulled her tighter into his arms.

"Honey, we all love you and want you to be happy. You have held yourself back for so long. You need to let go and let someone in who loves you -- and I think Austin's the gal for the job."

"Oh Oscar, I do want someone to love me. I'm tired of being alone."

"I know, darlin'. I know." They continued to hold each other, oblivious to the customers around them.

~~~~~

The next day Jaime arrived a few minutes before the doctor. "Good morning, how are you feeling?" She walked over to the bed and took hold of Austin's hand.

"I'm great, ready to get out of here. The doctor ought to be here soon." Austin wagged her finger at Jaime to come closer and as Jaime bent down, she pulled her in close for a kiss. The kiss started out slowly, two lips pressed together and then Austin let her tongue slip out and along Jaime's lips. Jaime sucked in her tongue and relished the excitement of things to come. They were so engrossed they didn't hear the doctor come in.

The doctor cleared his voice a couple of times. "Uh, excuse me, Ladies? Ladies?"

Jaime pulled away first and looked into Austin's eyes. They were burning with passion and Jaime knew her eyes looked the same. She leaned in and kissed her one more time and then pulled back. She continued to hold Austin's hand, not wanting to let go just yet.

"Sorry, Doc. I hope you've got good news." The doctor looked at both women with a red face.

"Yes, Ms. Stevens, I do, I'm letting you go this morning. The nurse will be by in a few moments with your release papers. Once you sign the discharge papers, someone from transportation will be by with a wheelchair to take you out. Ms. Crocket, you can pull your car around to the front, if you would like."

"Thanks, Dr. Brown. I appreciate your taking care of me." Austin stuck out her hand to the doctor.

"My pleasure and you take care. I want to see you in a couple weeks for a follow-up," he said as he shook Austin's hand.

"I'll make sure she gets here, Doctor." Jaime interjected before Austin said anything. She could see Austin getting ready to try to talk him out of a follow-up appointment. Austin looked at her with consternation on her face and then it softened, letting her know it was okay.

The drive back to the park was uneventful. When Jaime opened the door to Austin's RV, two little dogs were waiting there sitting in their usual spots, tails wagging.

"There's my babies. Did Jaime take good care of you? Of course, she did. Clara it looks like you've put on a little weight, have you been begging again?"

"She doesn't beg; she plays the cute card and I can't resist."

"Cute card, huh?"

"You know, where she looks at you and then rolls over on her belly shaking her little legs back and forth all the while wagging her tail, cute card. I can't resist."

"At least my boy doesn't do that." Rocky Bob looked at her with big brown eyes and rolled over on his back.

"Oh no, not you too," Jaime laughed and helped Austin on up into the RV.

"My gosh, this place looks different, what did you do?" the Amazon exclaimed as she looked around her place.

"Um, well, I washed the clothes, folded, and put them up. And basically, kept up with everything. I didn't really do much. I'm sorry we didn't get to eat your spaghetti sauce, but I'll take a rain check. I put what you made in a container and put it in your freezer." Jaime said as she walked around the front area making sure nothing was out of place.

"Well, the place looks great, thank you for staying with the pups. You can have a rain check anytime you want. In fact, you can have as many as you want." A rustling of a curtain told them Titus was about to make himself known. He stuck his head out of the curtain above the driver's seat and meowed.

"Hello there, big guy did you miss me?" Austin reached out to stroke his head, which he let her do and then he jumped down and proceeded to look at Jaime as if to say. "Now that I've had my pet, you need to let me out." Jaime walked to the door to open it.

"Oh yes, your majesty, anything you say, your majesty." Jaime opened the door and the cat leapt out and headed off toward the main part of the park swishing his tail in accordance with his standing in the park animal community. Austin chuckled and looked at Jaime. Jaime's eyes had deepened to a dark green and Austin felt her legs go weak.

She sank down to the floor and loved on both the dogs. As much as she wanted to be with Jaime, she needed to love on her best friends first. She spent a good twenty minutes, stroking and kissing them, telling them they were good babies and she loved them so much for finding her and saving her. They soaked it up, loving the praise from their mistress.

"Okay, you two, in your beds." The dogs looked at Austin and crawled into their beds. Jaime had mentioned she had let them out before she left to pick up Austin, and she knew they were going to be okay for a while.

Jaime was sitting on the sofa, watching Austin. Her eyes were focused, seeming to become more intense the more she looked at her. Austin raised her hand.

"Help me up?" Jaime got up, reached down and grasped both of Austin's hands. As Austin stood, she tugged her in close, looked into her eyes and then kissed her. It was a sweet, gentle kiss, reminiscent of the kisses she had with Maddie. Not expecting anything different, she was surprised when Jaime plunged her tongue into her mouth, trying to get as much of her tongue inside as possible. Austin groaned. Her arms went around Jaime and pulled her even closer.

She ran her hands up and down Jaime's body as she had done the other day in her daydream. Jaime followed suit, running her hands all over Austin. Their kissing became more intense the longer they stood there and although Austin was loving every minute of it, her leg was beginning to hurt.

Austin pulled away. "Okay to go to the bed?"

"Yes" was the only thing Jaime said. They walked back toward the bed, never letting go of each other. Austin felt her legs hit the mattress and she fell back with Jaime landing on top of her with a loud groan.

"You okay? I didn't hurt you, did I?" She was looking down at Austin's leg.

"No, Sweetheart, I'm good." If Jaime's look could have intensified any more, Austin felt for sure she would be burning up from the inside out.

"I need you naked, I want to feel you touching me." Austin nodded and Jaime helped her take off her top. She stared at Austin's breasts. They were firm but fell just a bit. Austin was worried Jaime wouldn't like them.

"Perfect," Jaime whispered as she leaned in, gently kissing each one, going back and forth, driving Austin mad. Then she took a nipple in her mouth scraping it with her teeth and biting down slightly. Austin writhed beneath her, grabbing her head and gripping her mouth onto her breast. Jaime moved to the next and did the same thing.

Austin could feel the heat rising from her body and wetness coating her legs. Jaime stopped her war on her breasts and made her way back up Austin's torso to her neck and face. She planted feather-light kisses all around the Amazon's face. She continued her onslaught, intensifying the worship by sucking and lavishing her with her tongue back down to her breasts where she seemed to stop.

Austin gasped, "Jaime, baby, I need . . ." but she couldn't go on. She was overwhelmed with the pleasure she was feeling throughout her whole body. Jaime finally moved and began to make her way down Austin's body, slowly kissing as she went, following a trail to Austin's sweet nectar.

Jaime slowly unzipped Austin's shorts and pulled them down along with her underwear, taking care not to rub her bandages from the bites. Once she removed the last bit of clothing, she kissed her way up Austin's legs, lingering on her wounds, gently kissing each one. As she moved up her legs, she spent time caressing and kissing, slowly making her way up the inside of her legs. As she got to her center, the shopkeeper slipped her tongue over Austin's clit, sucking and nipping, mimicking her earlier actions.

Austin bucked as she felt the first lash of Jaime's tongue. The shopkeeper's actions were sweet torture and she was overwhelmed. She couldn't speak, but felt everything. Jaime was touching her everywhere and then when she reached her clit, she thought she was going to orgasm right then and there, but Jaime wouldn't let her. She teased her with her tongue. Stroking her clit and then plunging into her center, stroking and plunging, it was driving Austin mad.

"Jaime, please, please, I want to feel you inside me." Jaime complied and added first one finger and then another in Austin's center. She kept rhythm with the stroking of her tongue, driving Austin higher and higher. Austin grabbed Jaime's head, entangling her fingers in her hair, holding her in place. All the while, Jaime was still plunging in and out, in and out.

She thought she was never going to reach the pinnacle and then she was rushing over, falling, trembling and exclaiming Jaime's name over and over. Jaime continued to stroke her and plunge into her, pulling her up to another orgasm. She didn't think she could experience another one, but she was wrong and was sent over the edge again, sending ripples through her whole body. Jaime slowed her actions, riding in and out on the waves and finally, when she was spent, Jaime slowed her rhythm and stopped.

"Amazing. I've never felt anything so intense," Austin said breathlessly.

"I'm glad I could please you, madam, I've been thinking about doing this to you for a while now." Jaime teased as she eased her fingers out and made her way up to Austin's mouth. She coated Austin's mouth with her own juices and then licked them off. Austin groaned with pleasure and drew Jaime in for a deeper kiss. They kissed and Jaime caressed her for a while longer. As she moved her fingers ever so lightly along Austin's body, she heard her lover's breathing even out and she knew Austin had fallen asleep.

Jaime lay next to Austin for a few moments, loving the feeling of having her next to her. She looked at her and realized she loved her. She didn't know a lot about this woman, but she knew she loved her and wanted to be with her the rest of her life.

"I guess it's true. When you know, you know," she said to herself as she, too, drifted off to sleep.

NEW LOVE

A couple of hours later, Austin awoke to find Jaime stroking her breast ever so lightly.

"I'm sorry did I wake you. I couldn't help touching you, I wanted to feel you." Jaime said as she continued to stroke her.

"Best way to wake up. I'm sorry I fell asleep, I guess I haven't totally recovered." Austin reached up and pulled the loving woman's head down for a tender kiss.

"No problem, I got what I wanted." Jaime grinned at her.

"Hmmm, yes you did, but what about what I want?" The Amazon pulled her down again and deepened the kiss.

After a moment, Jaime pulled back and said, "What do you want?"

Austin appeared to think for a moment and then she grinned salaciously. "I had this vision and I was hoping you would help me make my dream come true."

Her eyes turned to silver as she began to run her hands up and down Jaime's voluptuous body. Jaime closed her eyes and managed to say, "Sure, uh, oh my, what can I do?" The sensations Austin was creating were hindering Jaime's ability to think.

Austin moved her hands down to her hips and began pulling her up her body. "Move up and straddle my face."

Jaime looked at her with a surprised grin tempered with a look of overwhelming delight. "Oh, you are a naughty woman."

Jaime rose up on her knees and continued the climb to the top of Austin's head. She had removed her clothes before she snuggled into Austin for a quick nap. She looked down at Austin and lowered her center onto Austin's mouth. Austin's tongued flicked out and Jaime bucked. Austin grabbed her legs and held her down. Sucking and licking her clit, using her tongue to ram into her. Jaime tried bucking again, but Austin held her tight, taking her to new levels she had never been before.

"Oh. My. God. This is amazing, don't stop, harder, suck harder, yes that feels so good." Jaime kept talking to Austin, turning her on more and more as she talked.

As Jaime neared her orgasm, she yelled, "Inside me, inside me, fuck me, oh yes baby, keep fucking me."

Austin had not been with a woman like Jaime, she was so open and told her exactly what she wanted. Maddie had tried to talk dirty a few times when they made love but letting go of inhibitions was not in her nature. Austin could tell she felt uncomfortable in the early stages of their relationship and had stopped asking after a few times. She felt herself getting close to orgasm as she continued to do Jaime's bidding.

"I'm coming, oh baby, I'm coming." Jaime tried to rise but Austin held on to her, holding her legs tight with one arm, while the other one pumped her fingers inside her. She could see her lover squeezing the cushions on the headboard. Her hands were white from strain and as Jaime plummeted over into the abyss of her orgasm, Austin went over the edge with her.

After a few moments, Jaime lifted her leg and shifted down to lay beside Austin. "Oh, baby, that was so good. Thank you." She was breathless.

"No, thank you. I've never felt the passion I feel with you. You make me want to stay in bed with you all day and never leave." She gazed lovingly into Jaime's eyes, which had deepened to dark green, reminding her of the pools found in the deepest part of the forest.

"We don't have to leave the bed, at least not today anyway." Jaime giggled and snuggled into Austin, putting her head on her shoulder. Austin knew they had a lot to learn about each other, but they had time and she was so happy. She fell asleep again with the knowledge that she had found a home again.

They slept into the late afternoon and then only left the bed to let the dogs out to go to the bathroom and then they were back in each other's arms. As the evening progressed, Jaime found the courage to ask Austin about Maddie. "Austin, can we talk for a few minutes?" They had finished another round of satisfying love-making and the Amazon was running her hand up and down Jaime's body, caressing her.

"Sure, honey, we can talk about anything you want."

"I want to talk about Maddie." The caressing stopped for a moment and then began again.

"Okay, what do you want to know?"

"I want to know everything. Don't be mad, but your Dad told me about her yesterday before he left, but I wanted to hear what you had to say."

"Oh, gosh, Jaime. I don't know where to start. Maddie was in my life for over thirty years, there's too much to tell."

"Start at the beginning. Maddie was your partner and I know she is the reason you acted the way you did, but I can't commit myself to creating a life with you if I don't know who she was and what she meant to you."

"Creating a life with me, sounds amazing. Okay, Maddie was my savior. I know that sounds cliché, but it's true in every sense of the word. She saved me from myself. I was in so much trouble, mentally and physically."

"What do you mean, in trouble?"

"I was drinking too much and acting like women were there for one thing and one thing only, to please me. Maddie didn't buy it. She wasn't someone I could wrap around my finger and then discard. I tried, believe me I tried, but the harder I tried the more she pushed me away. Believe it or not, I was not a nice person when I was younger. I was angry at the world and I took my unhappiness out on everyone. Even my family."

"Why were you so unhappy? I've met your family; they seem like a loving bunch of people."

"Yes, they are and were, but I was mad. I was angry my mother was taken from me and my Dad tried, but I wanted my Momma. I was the only girl and I counted on my Mom to be there for me and with me. When she died, a little part of me died as well."

"Oh, Austin, I'm so sorry." Jaime pulled Austin into a hug, holding her tight, trying to show she was with her.

"No, don't be sorry. Maddie saved me in all the ways that someone who loves you can save you. She was patient with me and strong. She didn't put up with my bullshit. She told me everyone has a time on this earth and when their time is done, they must go. She said it was simple, it was my Mom's time to go and I had to accept it."

"She sounds very insightful." Jaime caressed Austin's face as she listened to her story.

"She was and I am so thankful she came into my life. I fell in love with her and we were together for thirty years. I loved her so much and I miss her every day. I've spent the last five years missing her and wishing she was here with me." Jaime didn't know what to say, as she didn't expect this kind of honesty. She lifted off Austin, trying to move off the bed, but Austin wouldn't let her go.

"Whoa, don't go. It's true I miss her, but I'm so glad I met you. I don't want to live my life alone. I want you, Jaime. I've wanted you since I first saw you. I didn't know what to do. I felt guilty for wanting you. I don't want to be alone anymore." Austin had tears falling down her cheeks as she looked into to Jaime's eyes. "I want you."

"Oh, Austin, I want you too, but I don't want to compete with a ghost. I want to be your one and only. I've waited so long for someone like you."

"Then don't wait any longer. I want you; I need you, and I, uh, oh, what the hell, I love you. I know this seems soon, but I knew when I saw you, we were meant to be together." Austin pulled Jaime closer, relishing the feel of the smaller woman's body against her.

"I love you, too. I don't usually let myself get this close to someone, but there's something about you Ms. Stevens. I want to throw caution to the wind and my internal voice be damned."

"I know what you mean, I want to feel love and passion and life again. I want you, Jaime Crocket, if you'll have me."

"Oh, I'll have you today and for the rest of our lives." Jaime leaned down and kissed her Amazon.

WEDDING DAY

The day was turning out to be gorgeous. The sky was clear and bright blue. The atmosphere at the park was festive. Decorations had been put up all around the area of Jaime's bookshop. A small pergola had been raised just outside the entrance. Chairs had been placed in front of the pergola, where all the guests would sit. A string quartet was tuning their instruments as they prepared to deliver the processional music.

Dallas and Oscar were standing on each aisle of the chairs to escort guests in as they arrived. Austin's other brother and his family were sitting on both sides of the aisle to show support for both women. Barney and Buckston were waiting at the edge of the pergola for their respective brides to walk down the aisle. Sarah and Junior were waiting with the men to act as maid of honor and best man.

"Come on, Honey, everyone's waiting." Austin beckoned, looking out the window from their new

RV. They had traded in Jaime's RV to get a bigger rig for them to live in and had kept Austin's for guests.

"I'm coming, give me just a second. It's not every day a girl gets married. Besides, you're not supposed to see the bride before you marry her." Jaime was finishing putting on the little bit of makeup she felt was required for this type of day.

"I don't believe in those old wives' tales and I want to give my girl a kiss before I make her mine officially." She leaned in, blocking Jaime's view of the mirror and kissed her gently.

"Now, are you ready?"

Jaime leaned into her forehead and whispered. "I am and I do until death do us part. I love you so much my Amazon and I love you for wanting to share your life with me. I am so thankful you shared your story of Maddie with me and that she gave you her blessing. I have loved sharing your world over the last eight months, getting to know you and be with you. I love your family and I am so glad they are my people too." She sealed her love for Austin with a passionate kiss, expressing everything she said by making a soul connection.

Austin reveled in the words and the soul kiss. She was home again. Maddie had been her first home, but she knew Jaime was going to be her forever home.

"I love you too, Sweetheart. You are my life and I never thought I would have a second chance at love. I thank the divine every day for your coming into my life and showing me love does come a second time around. Thank you for loving me!" Austin rose and held out her hand. Jaime took the outstretched hand and they came together for another searing kiss.

Jaime was dressed in cut-off jeans with a bright Kelly-green tank top that showed off her eyes. The best part was she had on a straw cowboy hat and green cowboy boots. Her hair was held back by the cowboy hat, but there were stray hairs here and there framing her face.

"You are so cute; I could eat you up." Austin said as she grinned at her lover.

"You did last night, baby doll." Jaime smirked as she took in Austin. She was wearing cut-offs with a blue tank top and blue cowboy boots. Her straw hat sat jauntily on her head and her head was still shaved to the shortest point without being bald.

"Are you ready?" Austin said as she opened the door.

"Yes, I am. Let's go have ourselves a party."
They walked hand and hand out of the RV. Each
woman was holding a leash with a little dog and a
big cat was walking in front of them. Austin knew
the second time around was going to be the best
time around.